Prais...

"Quickly, deftly, Strong lays out the financial, emotional and sexual complexities of the three marriages and draws each of the family members for us. . . . Part of the sense of life in the book comes from Strong's distinctive prose style—compressed, telegraphic and gestural, one in which the sharp noticing of what might otherwise seem like ordinary details about a character or an exchange takes on a resonating depth."

—*The New York Times Book Review*

"As artists and writers know all too well, there's no place like home for the holidays. . . . Lynn Steger Strong's slender but affecting new novel, *Flight*, ventures into this familiar terrain with a deft touch and an intuitive grasp of her characters . . . Strong is an exacting observer of families and their idiosyncrasies, in the mode of Anne Tyler and Jonathan Franzen. . . . Strong keeps *Flight* in motion with twists of language and revelation . . . More than just a domestic tale, it is a larger portrait of hearts and minds at war with the tedium of everydayness and the rote routines of relationships. . . . Grab a mug of egg nog, good readers, and dive in."

—*Washington Post*

"It's fall, season of Big Family Sagas, and Strong . . . delivers. . . . Pages [fly] quickly by as the story takes off."

—*Los Angeles Times*

"Richly painted and powerfully poignant."

—*Good Housekeeping*

"With deft, discerning prose, Strong writes beautifully about mothers and the struggles, fears, and joys of motherhood."

—*Kirkus Reviews*

"A fateful few days in the lives of two families becomes in Lynn Steger Strong's hands a clear-eyed examination of our current moment. *Flight* probes deeply into grief and its aftershocks, what binds us to one another, the meaning of art itself. It's a book whose fleet movements belie its ambition. Suspenseful, dazzling, and moving."

—Rumaan Alam

"Lynn Steger Strong is a master of family life, a wise chronicler of economic struggles real and imagined, of dreams versus responsibilities, and of nuances in relationships of all kinds. Arresting and powerful, *Flight* examines the possibility and pain of fierce love and hope in our time of looming existential threats."

—Lily King

"With razor-sharp pacing and luminous prose, Lynn Steger Strong aims her keen eye on the complexities of siblings, marriage, motherhood, and grief. *Flight* is a wonderfully alive look at the ways we try—defiantly and sometimes perilously—to love one another. You will want to gulp this book down in one sitting, but I urge you to slow down because its charms should be savored."

—Cynthia D'Aprix Sweeney

"Breathtakingly propulsive and insightful, *Flight* gripped me from the very first page and didn't let go. It asked my heart to pay better, closer attention to the world, because *it* pays such exquisite attention to the world: from botched gingerbread houses to cigarette breaks, every scene bristles and pulses with nuance. Strong is a writer who makes me feel reconfigured, more sharply attuned to the business of being alive, as if I have nerve endings that didn't exist before reading her. *Flight* is a story about how we lose and find one another again—and how this finding is never done, because we are, all of us, many selves at once."

—Leslie Jamison

"A gorgeous novel, both intimate and expansive. *Flight* is packed full of wisdom about family, marriage, class, climate, love, and loss. Lynn Steger Strong is a master of creating characters so funny, flawed, and true that they feel like people you know. I couldn't put it down."

—J. Courtney Sullivan

"In her brilliant new novel, Lynn Steger Strong reaches astonishing new depths of moral complexity in her depiction of family life in the aftermath of loss. Gripping, tender, and very funny, *Flight* proves once again that she is one of the great chroniclers of our strange and perilous times."

—Andrew Martin, author of *Early Work*

"Once again, Strong demonstrates her talents for perception and nuance."

—*Publishers Weekly*

"One of the best depictions of a family that I've read in a long time. . . . It would be a mistake to imagine this is *just* a story of parents and children. It is a story about how families shape our lives, even when we are away from them, and what happens when the natural order of the world is disrupted."

—Literary Hub

"[Strong's] characters feel both familiar and unique, and she is skilled at creating subtly devastating moments mixed with hope and tenderness. Written during a time of intense isolation, *Flight* reminds us that there is power in community, family, and those special times in which we don't have to do anything but be human."

—*Booklist*

"An intimate exploration of complicated family dynamics featuring nuanced portraits of distinct characters. It's a perfect book for anyone who feels more than a little conflicted about going to visit family for the holidays. With compassion and a deep sense of understanding, *Flight* explores the nature of belonging, and what it means to truly be part of a community."

—BuzzFeed

"A *Family Stone*–like turn."

—*The Hollywood Reporter*

"I am delighted to report that [*Flight*] was even better than I hoped. . . . This is the book to pack for any 'flight' you take this holiday season."

—*Good Morning America*

"Incredibly propulsive and filled with razor-sharp insights, Lynn Steger Strong shows us the power of familial love and care, which can support us through the plentiful failings of modern life."

—*Chicago Review of Books*

"Nuanced and multidimensional. . . . The myriad fissures, fractures and worries are what make this family drama feel utterly real."

—*BookPage*

FLIGHT

A Novel

LYNN STEGER STRONG

MARINER BOOKS

New York   Boston

HarperCollins books may be purchased for educational, business, or sales promotional use. For information, please email the Special Markets Department at SPsales@harpercollins.com.

A hardcover edition of this book was published in 2022 by Mariner Books.

FIRST MARINER BOOKS PAPERBACK EDITION PUBLISHED 2023.

Designed by Emily Snyder

Library of Congress Cataloging-in-Publication Data

Names: Strong, Lynn Steger, 1983– author.
Title: Flight : a novel / Lynn Steger Strong.
Description: First Edition. | Boston ; New York : Mariner Books, [2022]
Identifiers: LCCN 2022002946 (print) | LCCN 2022002947 (ebook) | ISBN 9780063135147 (hardcover) | ISBN 9780063135154 (trade paperback) | ISBN 9780063268555 | ISBN 9780063135178 (ebook)
Subjects: LCGFT: Novels.
Classification: LCC PS3619.T7785 F55 2022 (print) | LCC PS3619.T7785 (ebook) | DDC 813/.6—dc23
LC record available at https://lccn.loc.gov/2022002946
LC ebook record available at https://lccn.loc.gov/2022002947

ISBN 978-0-06-313515-4

23 24 25 26 27 LBC 5 4 3 2 1

For Luisa, Isabel, and Peter

We should insist while there is still time. We must
eat through the wildness of her sweet body already
in our bed to reach the body within the body.

—JACK GILBERT, "TEAR IT DOWN"

December 22: The Cars

TESS AND MARTIN

"You left them alone in the apartment?" Tess says.

"I'm downstairs, Tess. I'm right out front."

"And they're upstairs?"

They moved this year to a high-rise farther from the park but with a washer/dryer in the kitchen, a shared roof deck, a gym. Tess hadn't expected how scared she'd feel, being up so high. She searches from the sidewalk every weekday morning, walking to the subway, for their specific windows, not sure which of the apartments her children are still in.

"They're not babies," Martin says. "You're the one who wanted to leave by noon, then went to work."

"I still don't understand why we have to be gone so many days."

Martin's quiet. It's the twenty-second. Tess didn't want to go until the twenty-fourth.

"Did you pack the sweaters from your mother? All the presents? The kids can't see the Santa ones. Stell doesn't like the strawberry toothpaste; I have that little travel thing of Crest."

"I've packed for trips before."

"Your sister is going to want to take a thousand pictures."

"I packed for all of that."

"The pajamas she sent?"

"Yes. You left them folded by the door."

"Can you come get me?"

"You know I don't like driving in the city."

"We said we wanted to get there before dark."

"That was when you said you weren't going into work."

"Don't you think we need to make sure one of us still has a job?"

"Oh, fuck you, Tess."

"Can you please come pick me up?"

The street is quiet, wide and empty; so many of the cars already gone for the long holiday. Martin is surrounded by tall and glinting gray and widely windowed buildings, the one they live in indistinguishable from those on either side. He looks up to find their windows but can't quite.

He thinks briefly he might call his mother. He wouldn't talk to her about Tess, about their disagreement—they never talked much about Tess—he'd listen as she listed all the food she'd bought in preparation for the children, the meals and parties she was planning, baking slabs of gingerbread so that the kids could make houses, friends of hers who'd stopped by to bring gifts. She'd ask him what he thought about the side dishes, if she needed an extra pie because the kids were getting so big, the coffee Tess liked. She'd remind him to bring bathing suits and *something nice* for Christmas dinner, ask about the timing of their flight.

They're going to Henry and Alice's house upstate, though, not his mother's. Kate, her three kids, and Josh will meet them there. The three siblings—Martin, Kate, and Henry—they'll not be in Florida for Christmas for the first time in their lives because eight months ago their mother died.

KATE AND JOSH

"We should be hosting," Kate says.

They drive a dark blue van. It smells like pee and old bananas, a stale peanut butter sandwich. Josh drives, both hands on the wheel. Beneath Kate's feet is a stack of sweaters, backup toys, a cooler filled with snacks—hard-boiled eggs and cut-up fruit, carrot sticks and hummus, pretzels, Pirate's Booty. Behind them, all three of their children are on tablets with headphones. Bea, the oldest, plays a dragon game, her right index finger fast, up and down and sideways, on the tablet's screen.

"We don't have room for all those people," Josh says.

"Next year, we could . . ."

"I need you not to get your hopes up."

Whenever the topic of her mother comes up, he speaks to her as if she is a child. "Mom would have wanted the house to stay with us."

"She should have made a will, then."

Kate's mother died in May. She left behind her house and nothing else: the slow sludge of legalities right after; filing for the death certificate, waiting for the estate to clear. Martin's wife,

Tess, who is a lawyer, found a renter. They agreed to figure out the sale when they came together at Christmas. Which is now.

"I don't think she liked to think about leaving," Kate says.

"She left a mess instead."

Kate looks out the window. The sky is flat and gray. A bright orange square-shaped truck drives past. She thinks of crawling back into their van's third row to sit quietly with Bea.

"I watched this thing on YouTube about how to build an igloo," says her husband.

Behind them Jack grabs a chunk of Jamie's hair, and Jamie screams and swings his leg toward his twin.

"Both of you stop it!" Josh says, reaching behind his seat to grab Jack.

"Don't yell at them," Kate says, turning to touch Jamie. "Deep breaths, duck," she says to Jack. "Squeeze Mommy's hand."

He squeezes, and she hears him breathe and, she thinks, both of them feel better.

She faces Josh again, angry but not talking.

"They act like this because you don't discipline them," Josh says.

"Yelling isn't discipline. You have to talk to them."

"If you aren't quiet the rest of the drive, I'll tell Santa to forget the presents," Josh says, "no TV tomorrow."

"You can't threaten that," Kate says.

"They need consequences."

"Are you going to sit with them all day while I cook?"

Out the window, next to the highway, the trees are bare, and there's a light layer of snow on the ground. The road rolls and curves, and Josh keeps his eyes straight ahead. Kate presses her forehead against the window's cold and tightens her hand steadily on Jack's foot. She thinks how the foliage should be getting lusher, greener as they drive southward; the land should be flattening out instead of rising up in rocky jags. She thinks of all that warmth—how they should be changing halfway, at the rest stop, into shorts and T-shirts, letting the kids stay up late to go out to the beach as soon as they get there, to swim and wave-chase, feet dug deep in the hot sand. She thinks of the salt air and the smell of going outside barefoot, wet grass on her ankles, cradling her hot cup of coffee, sitting and talking every morning beneath the big banyan in her mom's backyard. Instead the air is getting thinner, sharper, outside her window; it all looks cold and dead.

She wants to ask her brothers to let her and her family live in their mother's house until her kids are off to college. They've always had money, Josh's inheritance. If this were two years ago, she'd just offer to buy her siblings out. But Josh went rogue and overinvested in a tech stock that tanked during the last recession. She thinks her brothers might be willing—she's the youngest. Ten years in which they can fix the house, up the value, sell and split the proceeds. A loan of sorts.

"Tess," she starts, already envisioning Tess's forehead creasing. Josh makes the face he makes when she says "Tess."

"I feel like Alice, even," she says, "might understand."

ALICE AND HENRY

"I thought maybe once she died I'd get Christmas," says Alice's mother on the phone from San Francisco.

Alice lights a cigarette, attaches and inserts her earbuds as she pulls out of the Food Town parking lot. "Mother, stop," she says.

"It's not like she might hear."

"You order in lo mein for Christmas."

"We order lo mein because we're all alone. Because our only child isn't here."

"We got Chinese food every year."

"The only ritual you ever cared about was that woman's."

"Mom. She's dead. You can say her name."

"*Helen*. Fine. You only ever liked Helen and her absurd, simplistic rituals; never me and mine."

Alice does not plan to but she turns left instead of right, down toward Quinn and Maddie's condo complex instead of back up toward her and Henry's house. She parks where she always parks, just out of view of their basement windows, pulls long on her cigarette. She can't see them; Quinn mostly keeps the curtains closed, but Alice still comes sometimes to sit, to look for them. Alice is Maddie's social worker. Quinn lost custody for six months after an accidental overdose, and it's Alice's job to check on them. She comes here more than to the other families she checks in with. Henry works out in the barn most of every day, and sometimes Alice drives around for hours; she parks out here, tries to get a glimpse of Maddie, as if her vigilance can keep her safe.

Quinn had work today, Alice knows, but Maddie had no school, and she thought maybe they might be here. But all the lights are off.

"Don't think I don't know what she thought," says Alice's mother, still talking about Helen.

Alice can no longer stomach her mother's truculence. "How's Dad, Mom?" she says.

"He's Dad."

"Is he home? Can I talk to him?"

"He's at work."

An older woman pulls into the spot next to Alice; Alice smiles at her and pulls out. She turns the car back up the long hill to the house. "Henry needs to be with his siblings this year," she says to her mother.

"Your whole life is built around what Henry needs."

"Please don't explain my life to me."

"I'm trying to make sure you get to live it."

"You mean like you did?" This is an old fight, too worn out to hit too sharply—shorthand for all the ways that neither woman would have chosen what the other has, for all the ways that neither of them is what the other might have wished she were.

"We'll see you on the twenty-eighth, then?"

"Henry has to work, but I'll be there."

"Did your husband get a job?"

"Henry's working on his work."

"So, then, he's available to come see us for a few days, because he does not get paid for what he does?"

"Can we please not do this?"

"I just think it's ridiculous that he's going to miss my New Year's party because he's building trinkets in the backyard barn that my dead mother made available to him."

"He's an artist, Mother."

"*You're* an artist, Alice. What has Henry ever done with his art?" Her mother says the word "art" like it's alleged.

"I'm not an artist anymore."

"Of course. A social worker."

"I have to go, Mom."

"The twenty-eighth, then, both of you. I'll send Dad to pick you up."

Alice feels too tired. "Merry Christmas, Mom."

"Of course."

When she gets back home she walks behind the house, leaving the groceries in the car. She watches Henry's shadow move as if suspended on the ceiling of the barn. He's built scaffolding to work up there, though they don't talk about what he's constructing. She thinks of going to ask him to come inside and sit with her—to hold her, help her. But she doesn't; she has a strange fear of going into this space that is now only his, this space she's not sure she believes in anymore. She lights another cigarette and checks her texts, hoping she might have one from Maddie. Just her sisters-in-law, though: Kate telling her she's bringing an extra air mattress, asking about blankets, whether or not she needs to bring more flour; Tess reminding her of Colin's peanut allergy. Alice makes a list, on her phone, of all the work she still has to do to make the house ready for Henry's siblings, takes a last drag of her cigarette, goes around to get the groceries from the car.

QUINN AND MADELEINE

"Walrus!" Quinn says. They pop both their teeth out of their mouths as if they're tusks, flap their arms and hands; they bark, twist their bodies like they're gliding on the ground.

They walk from Quinn's work, where they have gone together because there was no school and Quinn didn't have a sitter. Maddie sat for hours behind Quinn's law-office reception desk— while Quinn answered phones and greeted people, she read her book, then googled on the phone she got from the social worker when she got bored. Now they play the game they often play on their walk home, Animals. Maddie likes it because she loves animals, Quinn likes it because she likes being the sort of mom who will pretend to be a walrus or a horse out on the street regardless of the people who might watch.

"Spider," Maddie says, her words mangled because her teeth are still out of her mouth.

Quinn spreads her arms out wide over her head and straightens her back. Maddie goes on tiptoe, bringing her hands close to her chest, fingers working like they're weaving a web.

"Unicorn," says Quinn, and Maddie neighs and makes hooves

out of her hands; both of them prance, heads up high and bounding down the hill, rolling their necks.

"Dragon," Maddie says. They spread their arms. Maddie opens her mouth wide and hisses hot air from her throat, spitting fire.

"Octopus," says Quinn, and they both wiggle, loosening and rolling their bodies and their limbs. "Do octopuses—octopi?—make any sounds?" Quinn asks.

"Octopuses," Maddie says. "No sound."

They're almost home, off the main street. Quinn thinks she sees the social worker's car parked near their place, but then the car pulls out, drives off. Quinn squints but she can't tell if the car is Alice's; her eyes feel worn out from all the time in front of screens at work. She has two bags slung over the same shoulder: all the snacks she packed for Maddie, the books she brought, her wallet, keys, and phone. They pass an older couple, and Quinn stops wobbling her limbs as she notices them watch her and Maddie too close, too long—looking. *Imminent danger,* she thinks, which is the language that they used the first time they took Maddie from her, the language that runs through her brain a thousand times a day.

"Peregrine falcon!" Maddie says—her favorite. The couple has walked past them. The path is straight down a hill, the sidewalk cleared of snow, and both Quinn and Maddie spread their wings out wide and high and fly straight down.

The House

A foot of snow's stuck to the ground, and the last bit of sun still glints along the wide white fields. Mountains loom behind: a mess of rock and branches, overlapping trunks, mixed with long patches of white. Tess and Martin drive past the Hudson, up the last long hill, toward Alice and Henry's house. Tess looks back at the kids, Stella six and Colin almost nine; they're too old to nap but they've passed out, and now they'll wake up grumbling, hungry, less prone to sleep at the actual right time tonight. Tess catches sight of Kate's van as Martin puts the car in park—Virginia plates, the back piled haphazardly with stuff—and her neck and shoulders clench. She loves but does not like Kate. She often fantasizes about maiming Josh.

Tess reaches into the back seat to collect the trash from the children's snacks, to pack the books and tablets from beneath their feet into a canvas bag. "We should have left earlier," she says to Martin.

"We're here now," he says.

The house is old and rambling, two stories, chipped white paint, smoke coming from the chimney. Tess looks back again at the kids, still and quiet as they almost never are. She wishes this visit were already over, that they could all be heading back, grateful for the efforts everybody made but relieved to once again be separate. She steels herself instead for all the time they will have together, the forced acts of being a large extended family, something for which she feels constantly so ill-equipped.

She says: "We sure are."

"Deep breaths," Martin says, half joking, *trying*. Martin, who is good and steady, a solid partner, has been called up on review by the university where he was—still is, for now—a full professor. He's been forced to take a leave as of this month, and he's less prone right now to look straight at Tess when they talk.

Tess laughs at him. "I'll get Stell," she says, opening her door.

Both the children are too big to be carried, but Tess whispers her daughter's name as she unhooks her from her seat. Stella mumbles, opens her eyes, looks at Tess, and settles herself more firmly into her mother's arms. Her face and back are wet with sweat, chin-length dark hair stuck to her cheeks. The weight of her is warm and solid, and Tess thinks she might hold Stella like this the whole time that they're here.

Colin stirs, face slack, skin splotched. He has the same dark hair as his sister, cropped close to his head because he can't sit still enough to get any cut besides a full-headed, thickly clippered buzz. He shoots both arms over his head. "My neck hurts!"

"You just have to move," Tess says. "Get out and stretch."

Martin steps out of his way as Colin climbs out of the car. He's big all of a sudden, Colin. The top of his head reaches almost to Tess's shoulder, and he talks to her as if he doesn't quite believe she should be trusted. She wants to walk over to him, brush the wet red of his cheek, rub her thumb along his neck. But she does not.

The yard's covered in snow, thicker than it looked from the car, and Tess thinks she should find Colin's boots in the trunk before his shoes get soaked, but he's already bounding toward the house. Tess follows close behind with Stella in her arms.

The mudroom is made up almost completely of large windows, an unfinished wood floor. Boots and coats are piled on a bench that Henry built, which takes up one whole wall and half of another. Snowshoes sit crooked in the other corner, a couple sleds—and Alice and Henry are at the door. Alice reaches down and wrestles with Colin's laces, gets his shoes off, stands and hugs him, holds him. Colin's arms and back stay stiff.

"Hey, kid," Alice says.

"Hey, Aunt Alice," Colin says.

Henry grabs him quickly by both shoulders. "You must get that height from someone other than your dad."

Tess watches Colin avoid eye contact with Martin. He smiles at his uncle and runs into the house to find Kate's kids.

"A couple of years up here and now you're into sports?" Tess says, nodding toward the sleds.

Alice smiles at her. "You've been in the city so long you think sleds are sports?"

When Alice and Henry still lived in the city, Tess and Alice used to meet for coffee in the middle of the workweek. They weren't close, but the regularity of their meetings made their interactions feel more solid to Tess then. She liked to listen to

Alice talk about art, her friends and colleagues; liked the way her whole world felt separate from what Tess had always thought she wanted, how she thought she had to live. Tess would always be a little bit embarrassed—sitting in the downtown coffee shops that Alice frequented, close to the studio where Alice rented a small space to paint and show her work to gallerists—by the stolidity and sameness of her suits.

Now they talk a couple times a month, they text.

"We got them for the kids," says Henry.

Tess watches Alice, whose face stays placid. Alice and Henry don't have children, though they tried for years.

Martin comes through the door with the first round of bags, and Stella slips out of Tess's arms, pulls off her shoes, quickly hugs her aunt and uncle. "Keep an eye on those big kids for me, will you?" Henry tells her.

Stella smiles at her uncle. "Got it," she says.

"This hair is perfect for this face," says Alice, coming toward Stella.

Martin sent a picture last week on the family group text (Tess seldom sends texts on the family group text)—new haircut: Stella with blunt bangs and her hair chopped to her chin.

Stella reddens, hand to her hair, dutifully says thank you. Alice lets go, chastened; Stella bounds into the house.

"Can I help?" Henry asks. He's a broader version of his brother. Two inches taller. The same strong jaw but wider, a flatter, less long nose.

Martin nods, hands him the keys. Henry heads out to the car.

"How's it going?" Tess asks Alice.

"Great," says Alice, her eyebrows raised and her lips scrunching. Her hair's cut close, and her sweater is dark blue, long and drapey; Alice holds it, wrapped over both sides of her waist, as she talks. She's beautiful, Tess thinks each time she sees her. When they met for coffee, Tess almost always got there first, and she would watch Alice come in from across the room and wonder what it might be like to look like that; saw the way other people looked at Alice as she walked by them, the power she must have. She has light brown skin, dark eyes. They're all in their forties, but Alice—her skin so smooth that Tess used to worry she wouldn't be able to help herself, would reach out to touch it—could easily be mistaken for twenty-five.

Now Tess laughs and holds Alice's arm close to the elbow. "*Great*," she says.

"Josh is building an igloo," says Alice.

Tess lines each kid's set of shoes along the wall behind them, hangs up their coats. "Of course he is."

Josh has a trust fund and often does things like this: well intentioned, at the same time useless and infuriating. They talk about Josh sometimes, Martin and Tess, Henry and Alice; it's a sort of sport among them to laugh about their sister's husband, *in good fun*.

It's not your job to like him, Helen would say when she caught them. Eventually she relented, agreed, *Sure, he's not ideal, but isn't everyone infuriating.* And then she would eye them in the way that only she could eye them. *It is your job to be his family,* she'd say.

"For the children," Alice says now, about the igloo.

"An *experience*," Tess says.

Tess should not take this all so personally, says Martin. He thinks she takes lots of things too far. What does it matter, Josh? But Tess can't help it. Josh does these things instead of helping with the children, cleaning up after lunch or dinner, noticing his wife's recent descent into depression, making any effort at his job. He is not productive or responsible. And Tess has built a whole life around the idea that if she stops being productive and responsible, even for a second, she'll die.

A muddled whiskey drink sits in a large pitcher on the thick wood counter, and Alice pours out one for each of them. "Holiday whiskey punch?"

Tess takes hers and thanks her, holds her arm again for no good reason. "Where's Kate?"

Alice nods toward the living room, but Tess doesn't move.

Kate hears them but she doesn't go to greet them. She wants a few more minutes alone, quiet. She's been working on the tree nearly since she and Josh and the kids got here, brought ornaments, most of them her mother's—she was the only one who wanted what Tess called the "holiday debris" when they emptied her mother's house. She thought she'd cry while she was hanging them but she hasn't so far. She's brought a fresh roll of garland she spent a whole evening making while Bea watched TV and the twins wrestled on the floor. They tried to staple the paper with her, but they ripped it and got frustrated and she was upset that the circles weren't the way she liked them, so she turned on the TV and made the garland by herself.

Two weeks ago, she made Henry and Alice send her a picture of the tree. She told them it was to gauge the size to know how many lights to bring, but really, it was to prove they had gotten it. She knew better than to depend on Henry for too much.

Colin bounds through the room. He brushes up against the tree, and the branches rustle, and she reaches out to grab and hug him.

"Hi, Aunt Kate," he mutters.

She brushes her head briefly against his. He's only two years older than her boys but is fully a foot taller. His face, stark beneath his tight-cropped hair, looks so much more formed than theirs.

"Where's Bea?" he says.

She nods toward the stairs.

"So big," she whispers, though he's gone already when she says this. She adores her nephew. His conversation is more grown up than her kids'; when he hugs her, he hugs longer and tighter, lets her breathe him in as often and as long as she wants. Though he can also be intense, intractable, can get frighteningly excited—he often drives Josh nuts.

She hears Tess laugh in the other room and feels the sides of her jaw tighten at the prospect of her quiet judgment, the way she always seems so sure she knows what's best. All Kate wants is a nice Christmas for the children, a few pictures, to not think only about how her mom being gone makes her feel sad and scared and like maybe she's being suffocated slowly, like she's falling from some high-up, cracked and broken cliff. They have to talk about the house, and Kate does not want to talk about it. She wants her brothers to look at her and see she needs it, to intuit, without her and Josh having to admit it, that they are running out of money. She wants them to feel somehow that she's not happy in Virginia—she no longer remembers why she thought she'd like living in Virginia—to suggest, without her having to ask, that she and her family take the place until her kids are grown and gone. This will not happen, of course. Not least because of Tess.

The tree, though, is nearly perfect. Kate has spaced almost all the ornaments the way her mother taught her. She strung the lights up first, and they loop up in a pleasing, bright white curve. There is the proper balance of the homemade and the store-bought, these truly awful bells she got for her mother at a school sale, ceramic, too white, with tiny bright red balls inside that no longer make much noise. She sees, has seen for years, that her mother kept them only not to hurt her feelings. Kate touches one of the clay angels that were her mother's favorite: not too big, intricately painted, passed down from Kate's grandmother. Up close, she sees one of its wings has broken, chipped off. She runs her thumb along the spot where it's missing, blank beige and sharp along the edges; she feels, all of a sudden, as if the tears might finally come.

"Drink?" she hears behind her. It's Alice—her big dark eyes, her hair cut close, her perfect face. Kate likes her more than she likes Tess. Tess is controlling and judgmental. Mostly, though, she dislikes Tess because Kate's mother loved her unreservedly.

"It's delicious," Tess says, as she comes up behind Alice.

They half hug one another. *So thin,* Kate thinks. When Tess met Kate's brother two decades ago, she hugged no one; *doesn't know how,* Helen used to say, before she decided that she liked her. All the warmth of which Tess is now capable, Kate feels sure, has come as a direct result of her relationship with Kate's mom.

"Looks nice," Tess says. She wears gray jeans and a black sweater, expensive looking.

"Thanks," says Kate. She watches Tess lean closer to the ornaments. *She must not eat,* her mother used to say. Her collarbones jut up; the edges of her wrists. She keeps her hair pulled back tightly from her face; *severe,* her mom used to say. *She doesn't quite have the face to pull it off.* Tess's eyes are small, her lips too thin. She always seems to like Kate best when she first sees her, when neither of them has said or done much yet.

A couple of years ago Tess ran the New York marathon, and Kate tracked the little GPS dot on the phone app. Kate had been exhausted by it, watching—while she made dinner, cleaned out the last of the summer clothes in the kids' closets—all that time not stopping (negative splits! Martin texted the family group text later), that little ceaseless dot.

"I brought dresses," Kate says now, attempting to feel festive. She lets go of the angel with the chipped wing, has to work hard not to grimace as it clanks against another ornament. "And little bow ties for the boys. I thought we could get a Christmas picture."

"Sure," Tess says. She sets her drink down, not smiling. Alice looks out one of the windows toward the snow.

Martin dated lovely women before Tess. All Kate's girlfriends had crushes on him. Some had maybe only come to Kate's middle school birthday parties to get a glimpse of him; he was tall and handsome. Tess was nothing like the girls who came before. She was sharp and hard and quiet, not at all the sister Kate had hoped for when she imagined Martin getting married. It's so much clearer to her now that none of them are what she hoped they would be. But Tess and Martin, Alice and Henry, whatever becomes of the children—they are all that she has left.

"You need help with the tree?" Tess says.

There's one box left. Tess isn't mean, she's just uptight. Kate has always liked her best when they're alone and after a few drinks. Often, in their twenties—Tess and Martin have been together since Kate was still in college—they'd run out of things to talk about and ended up talking shit: about Tess's sisters, who Kate knew Tess didn't like; about Helen, who asked too many questions, demanded they get dressed up when they didn't want to, corralled them into the kitchen to cook, though Tess can't cook, to *just be present for the party,* when neither of them felt quite up to it; about the men, such safe, easy targets then. And then Kate said something too harsh about one of Tess's sisters; Tess said something condescending about Helen's party making, and their burgeoning relationship would stutter to a halt. When they had kids, they suddenly had plenty to talk about again: the endlessness of sleep and food and schools and siblings. They're closer now, Kate likes to think, because of this.

Alice doesn't have kids but Kate finds her softer, less condescending and controlling. At Helen's funeral, it was Alice who took Kate's kids out for ice cream, let them run an hour on the beach so that Kate could cry on top of the covers in Helen's bed by herself.

It's as if neither of them, Alice nor Tess, knew what family was before they married Kate's brothers. Alice is an only child, which Kate figures is not her fault; the art stuff made Kate worry that all the ways she likes to decorate her home, likes the children to be dressed up at family get-togethers, would be garish, maybe childish, to Alice, as she imagined they were to Tess. But Alice always made small efforts: complimented Kate's and the kids' outfits, bought Kate serving platters and artisanally made bowls in the same colors as Kate's china.

"Help would be great," Kate says to Tess and Alice, nodding toward the box of ornaments and old tissue paper. Helen re-used wrapping paper, gift bags, so as not to waste but also to save money. Once Henry became obsessed with climate, Helen claimed that as a reason too.

The ornaments that are still left are all nearly falling to pieces— a cardboard circle painted by a seven-year-old Martin with his picture on it, smiling, front right tooth missing, *Merry Krsmas* scrawled in red beneath his smiling face.

"He looks like Colin," Alice says, fingering the picture.

"Colin looks like him," says Tess.

They look at the tree as if it is some strange beast that's just formed before them.

"Where does it go?" asks Tess.

"Wherever you want," Kate says.

She watches both Alice and Tess as they move between the box and the tree, tentative and careful. Helen wasn't religious. But some years she dabbled in Eastern religions of all kinds, made everyone meditate. Other years, she made them go to church *for the community*. She believed in parties, food, coming together— naming ceremonies instead of baptisms, Michaelmas some years, solstice parties—December twenty-first and Helen calling everybody back together early, a fire in the backyard and making resolutions late into the night—midsummer celebrations, birthday parties with too-big cakes and preordained themes. There was value in coming together, Helen said.

Now Kate knows it's her job to give this to her children. She does not believe in heaven or hell, ghosts or spirits, but she does believe, there or not, Helen will know if Kate doesn't keep all of this up.

She lets Tess and Alice place the last few ornaments. They're careful with them. Alice, who is the tallest, stands on tiptoe to fill the spaces that Kate's missed. Tess holds a handful of silver bells and lays them over a thick branch, both hands, careful. She looks at Kate as if for her approval, stands back.

"I can turn the lights on?" Kate says.

"The lights," Tess says. "Of course."

Kate crawls behind the tree to reach the outlet. Her shirt rides up and she imagines Tess seeing her belly, the way her ass looks in her jeans that have, in the months since Helen's death, become too tight. She plugs in the lights and stands up, steps back. The whole tree is bright and brilliant. Helen would be proud.

Alice takes a picture, which surprises Kate but is pleasing. Tess stands still and smiles, her eyes maybe wet. Kate takes a picture too, posts it to Instagram.

"It's lovely, Kate," Tess says, both hands in her back pockets.

Behind them they hear Stella cry. Tess starts, heads toward the stairs. Kate stays frozen, nervous, certain that whatever's happened, her kids will be found to be at fault.

"It's already starting," Alice says to Henry, escaping back into the kitchen.

She texts the picture of the tree to Maddie. She thinks of where Maddie might be in the condo: reading on the couch, watching TV, sitting close to Quinn. The phone that Maddie has is one that Alice gave her, an iPhone that Henry tried briefly but didn't like. That Alice still pays the bill is something that she figures Quinn must know but no one talks about.

"What?" asks Henry, who is already looking out the window toward the barn. Henry is never wholly present when he's not working. Alice understands this, though she sometimes wishes there were more space for her, too, to disappear herself.

"Your sister," she says. "One of the boys hit Stella, and now Tess is threatening to go home."

"She won't do it," he says.

"Her precious babies," Alice says, though she likes Tess. She likes Kate too. Mostly, she wants all the kids to stay so she can let them crawl up on her lap one by one and breathe them in.

"She'll calm down," says Henry. He nods toward the half-empty punch pitcher on the counter. "Bring her more of that?"

"You can't work tonight," Alice says. "Just so we're clear: you can't leave me until everyone is safe in bed." The house is drafty, its heating faulty. Alice started a fire to warm it up before the kids arrived. She chopped extra wood, sweating in her coat and cashmere sweater; they already had plenty, but she wanted to move, breathe hard, before the mess of them bore down.

In summer, Alice has a small garden out back. She likes to show the children, let them taste test the tiny berries, kale and mint and basil. Tess and Martin have been up a handful of times since Alice inherited the house. Growing up, Alice flew alone from California for a week or three in summer while her parents went somewhere far away and fancy—a Tahitian cruise, Nice and Biarritz and Paris. Her grandma, Elinor, thrice divorced and widowed, didn't seem much interested in Alice, though unlike at home in San Francisco, where she and her mother mostly ate at the kitchen counter with the TV on while her dad worked, they ate all their meals together in the dining room. During the day Alice wandered out back in the woods—at six and seven, fifteen—a little shocked each time she went out farther, sunburned and mosquito bitten, to find her way back to the house before dark. For all Elinor's indifference toward Alice, she'd actively disliked Alice's mother, and so Alice had inherited the house.

It was Henry's idea to move, but it was Alice who made it happen. This was often true for them. Henry thought of something, wanted something, and Alice executed it. Henry made work, but dinner, money, the deployment of any major life decisions, that was mostly Alice's job. This Christmas, just like every other Christmas since they got together, she was the one to purchase and to wrap all his family's gifts. She's stocked the pantry with the kids' favorite foods, processed snacks that Henry hates the wrappers and the waste of; she has the coffee each of his siblings likes, extra blankets on the beds for when the house gets cold at night. She has been a good wife to Henry and to Henry's siblings and their families; the least he can do now is not leave her alone with them.

He wraps his arm around her waist and brings his lips close to her cheek. He has a three-day beard, almost always. His eyes are, like his mother's and his brother's and his sister's, a light, yellow-flecked brown. Alice doesn't flinch or pull away, though that's her impulse. She's not sure she remembers the last time their bodies touched like this.

"They haven't even started to talk about the house."

"You scared of Tess?" he says.

"Absolutely. Both of them."

He loosens his grip, and she steps farther from him. She always wanted to be a woman who was friends with other women, but it didn't take. She tried to have female friends, but women never seemed to want to trust her, regardless of what she did or said. She had no siblings, no sisters to show her what it was like. And boys always liked her; it took her a long time to realize all the ways this made it harder for her with girls. Now, where they live, up in the woods, she often goes weeks without being looked at the way she used to be. She doesn't mind this, kind of likes it. She'd hoped, at her new job, to make more female friends, but the women there are older, all white. In her whole life Alice has only had two close Black female friends; both of them live far away and are that specific *always busy* that comes with little kids. Her colleagues are cordial to her during working hours, though when she sees them around town and smiles at them, they often do not smile back. Tess was almost her friend, when they lived in the city. But she's different, less accessible, when they're all mixed up like this.

"Seriously," she says to Henry. "You cannot leave me with them."

"I want to finish so the kids can see it," he says.

"They won't get it," she says, just to hurt him. The ease with which he leaves her, the ease with which he continues to believe his work has worth: she feels both anger toward him and a not-small amount of shame on his behalf.

"It's birds," he says, inured to her. "What's not to get?"

He's making them in clay, his birds: there's a kiln out back, and then he paints them. She knows because she smells it, because she saw him wheel the kiln from the back of his truck into the barn; she's not been out there since he started, a few weeks after they moved here. She hasn't asked, nor has he offered. They used to talk so much about work—form, material, shape, and execution; now that she doesn't make things, feels mortified, in fact, about the years she spent obsessed like him, she's not sure how they'll fill up all the days together they have left. Sometimes it's useful to her, reminding herself to still love him, to think about his fingers forming tiny feathers on the birds' small wings; to imagine the care it must take—she has no idea their size or what they look like—cupping their weight, holding them at different angles, still and careful and considering.

For years, both before and after she stopped making art, Alice was a person devoted wholly to the conceiving of a baby, and this depleted what little savings they had managed, along with whatever gestures of generosity her mother was willing to offer, and now Alice is sad a lot.

"I want you to see it too," Henry says.

His body is still close to her and he smells of sweat, paint, cumin, and parsley.

"You can't work until every one of them is safe in bed," she says a second time.

"We can't have just gummies for dinner," Quinn says. They've walked up to the Food Town to get groceries. There's a path straight from their condo complex, behind the main street, and it is safe and quiet, even after dark. Halfway up the hill she thought she saw her ex-boyfriend. She often thinks she sees her ex-boyfriend. He lives two towns over. She watched Maddie's posture, tried not to look straight at him, thinking maybe, almost certainly, she must have been mistaken. She tried to move her body in a way that proved how strong she is all by herself.

Quinn speaks loudly now for the same reason, walking through the Food Town. She wants the people in the store to hear how sweet and funny and responsible she is.

"Pasta," Maddie says. "And Parmesan. The good butter's on sale."

Quinn loads the cart with frozen vegetables and chicken fingers; they get a large bag of the Pink Lady apples Maddie loves. Quinn selects bread and cheese and sliced salami, mayonnaise. She got paid this week, and the holiday is coming, and she lets Maddie pick three pints of ice cream—cookie dough, cookies and cream, and chocolate—because the Häagen-Dazs is three for ten.

"Madeleine!" they hear behind them. Quinn turns to see a little girl with short hair and bangs, big eyes—a kid from Maddie's class. She approaches with her mother, an older kid beside her, a baby—fat legs sticking out from the hard wire—in the cart.

"Rosa!" Maddie says. "Hi!"

Quinn smiles at the other mother, who is stout and pretty, her hair cut short like her daughter's. "Hi," she says.

"You all headed out of town this week?" the mother says.

Quinn hasn't met her, she doesn't think, but is relieved this other mother doesn't mistake her for the babysitter or Maddie's older sister—Quinn is twenty-three and has been told that she looks younger.

"We're staying put," Quinn says.

"Oh God, us too," says this other mother, nodding toward her overflowing cart. "I'm hosting my entire family. The first time."

Quinn nods, smiling. Maddie is her entire family; she is Maddie's. "Sounds exhausting," she says.

"Stocked up on Ativan," the other mother whispers to Quinn as the baby starts to fuss. Quinn laughs and looks around to make sure no one's looking, no one heard this other mother whisper to her about a substance Quinn can't have in her home or she will lose Maddie for good.

"Smart move," Quinn says. She grabs Maddie's arm, Maddie waves goodbye to her friend, and as they turn down the nearest empty aisle, Quinn throws a bag of $5.99 organic chocolate chips into the cart.

2

Tess holds Stella in the kitchen.

"She's fine," Martin says for the thousandth time. He's standing too close to her. "Let her play."

Tess carries Stella over to the counter, pours her daughter and herself a glass of water. Stella's bangs are stuck crooked on her forehead—they paid too much for this haircut—and Tess brushes the thick, dark strands back. There is no bump or bruise or cut, but she was crying.

"They have no control," she whispers to her husband. "No one watches them." For a while, parenting brought her and Kate closer, but then Tess began to worry about Kate's kids' influence. The chaos of them, up close, made her afraid. Colin is so easily spun out. He's more violent, she thinks, after he spends time with his cousins. Every time.

"They're kids," says Martin.

"Want to help Uncle Henry cook?" she says to Stella. Stella loves her uncle.

But Stella shakes her head. "Can I go help Uncle Josh?"

Out the window they can see him, though it's dark now. He has a shovel, large waterproof black mittens. Josh is thin, wiry—not as fit as Martin, nor as tall as Henry. His hair, Tess thinks, is too long for a grown-up. Strands of it fall out of his hat into his face.

Tess watches as he packs the snow into bricks and piles one after the other. "It's too cold, honey."

"I have a coat."

"Can you please stay here?"

"Help me, Stell Bell," says Henry. It's hot in this room, the woodstove burning, and he wears a T-shirt, his face a little sweaty and splotched red. He takes Stella from Tess and puts her to work kneading the tortilla dough.

Tess sips her drink and pours herself a little more. She loves Henry with the exact same intensity that she hates Josh, though she didn't always. He seemed so young when she first met him, almost unformed, though he was, in fact, closer to her age than Martin was. Tess hadn't even known not to laugh when he first told her he was an artist. *I'm an artist interested in climate,* he had said—twenty years ago, Tess hadn't known what "climate" might possibly have to do with "art." What she knows now is he makes art that engages with what the climate was and what it isn't any longer, what it will never be again. In the barn, he's constructing a flock of birds across the length of the ceiling because soon, he's told her, flocks of birds won't exist in the way they always have. He's also told her that soon there will be no olive oil left in Italy, that coffee and chocolate plants need twenty-one straight days without rain to set and flower and soon such places won't exist. Efforts are being made to preserve the idea of them, the look and taste and smell of each these things; descriptions of the experience are being written down in order that the memory, at least, of what they were remains.

All she does is go to work, he texted about Alice last week.

That's all *you* do, Tess said.

We used to work *together,* he said.

I think the job is saving her, she texted back.

After she got over the initial shock, the strangeness of knowing working artists, for years Alice and Henry seemed magic to Tess, otherworldly. Tall, lithe, gorgeous Alice. Bearded, adolescently dressed Henry. They *made art* and had a tiny studio in Greenpoint. They had no health insurance, no real jobs. Tess, born of and bred by devoted capitalists, could not have fathomed choices like this. She found them silly sometimes, the sort of entitlement they must have: to think they had a right to live like this. Henry more than Alice; in part, Tess thinks, because Henry's a man, in part because Alice is half Black. Her mother, who mostly raised her, while her father worked and traveled nonstop, is white. And Alice's mother—the way she less looks at people than appraises, the way all her sentences feel clipped in ways that suggest she is deigning to keep certain things to herself—she reminds Tess often of her own mother. Tess and Alice are separate, different, from their husbands and their family, because they weren't loved and coddled, *nurtured,* the way Martin and his siblings always were.

The year Tess stopped talking to her mother—because she finally decided that it wasn't worth it, because she was too exhausted to keep trying, to prove she was not the sort of person who might break her parents' hearts—was the year Stella was born. She had a baby and a toddler. Henry would come pick up her and Stella from their apartment. Helen had come to stay with them for four weeks to help out but had had to fly back home for work. Tess's firm was ruthless, tough, but also, three of the partners were mothers, and all the women were given four months paid leave. Martin was in his last stretch of applying for tenure and was uptown at work more than he'd ever been. Tess was home alone all day and—though no one ever would have thought it; though the house was perfect every night, the dinner cooked (though pre-prepared by Martin), the rooms ordered, clean; though she checked in daily with the office; and though Stella nursed well and napped for long stretches and they had a nanny part-time for Colin—she'd still thought, in those four months, that she might go insane.

But Henry came a couple times a week and took her and Stella to galleries in Chelsea. Often, he would wear the baby for her. They didn't speak much. She thought Helen had called him to come look after her. They walked for hours, and he was smart and charming, funny. An almost wholly different being from Martin: he talked less, paused a long time before he answered any of her questions; *what is it you do, though,* was the thing she never had the courage quite to ask him. But she understood more, she thought, after all that time they spent together, the way he looked so long and careful, not just at the art but on the street. The way he was so steady, the whole time, the way, every time they saw a flock of birds swoop in between a stack of buildings or over their heads as they were walking, he would take her hand or grab her elbow, he'd pull Stella up out of the stroller to make sure that she could see.

Henry texts her about his art now, and she is actually interested after these years of friendship. Sometimes, about every other week, on her way back to the office between meetings, Tess sneaks into MoMA to look at art and try to see whatever Henry and Alice see. Her favorite is Alberto Giacometti, "Annette," a small portrait of a woman sitting straight in a chair, sharp and ghostly, grays and blacks and browns, blurry up close. She stares at Annette, often for too long, often late then for whatever meeting she has scheduled after lunch. Tess is a litigator, sharp and quick. But after these museum visits she feels less invested in pretending that any of what she's fighting for or against has any real-life stakes.

Tess hadn't realized how much she'd miss Alice and Henry now that they're no longer in the city: the strange elaborate meals they used to cook, their muddled drinks. She hadn't realized that Alice and Henry are the only people she and Martin spend time with who aren't like them.

She watches Josh pack one more brick. "Martin," she says. "Can you come here?"

"What's up?" her husband says. He's wearing one of Henry's aprons. He is chopping onions carefully, precisely—his mother's son, he has a perfect dice.

"Can you check on Colin?"

"He's fine, Tess."

"I'd just like you to check on him."

"Jesus, Tess."

She looks at him. She's using this small thing she has to use against him—the charges, which she's sure are bullshit, which even his bosses admit are absurd but still, right now, he feels bad about. She'll use this to get him—this whole weekend, maybe for all the years to follow—to go make sure the kids are safe.

As she sips her drink, Kate walks around trying not to envy the size of the house. She ignores the sound of the children fighting on the mattress on the floor in the room where she and Josh and their three kids will sleep. The upstairs bathroom's large, with an old claw-foot tub with a shower rigged on top; a space heater in the corner whirs. She opens all the drawers and runs her hands over their contents—ovulation strips, tubes of mascara, dried-out foundation rounds. Kate's the only one of the three women who wears makeup on the weekends. In the medicine cabinet: ibuprofen, lip balm, a line of lotions, that all-natural deodorant that is the reason Henry always smells. There's a whole hall wall of linen closets, mostly empty: threadbare towels and summer sheets. She takes a pile of extra blankets for the kids.

Of course the place is only this big because they're so far up here. She looked it up online when Henry and Alice first moved, the square footage and the pricing. She imagines the schools aren't any good. Alice has told her about some of the clients that she deals with as a social worker—opioids all over. Kate can't be picky about their house's size because she doesn't work. She did once, but Josh stopped her. Though that's *her narrative*, he says.

When they found out the twins were twins it hadn't made sense for both of them to work. Even though Kate made more, Josh would never be the one to stay at home. It wasn't really about the money, couldn't only be about the money. Kate was afraid of his not knowing what to do, his forgetting—to pick them up, to feed them, to pay attention, all the things she does. Kate had never loved her job; she loves the time she gets with her kids, though this is not something she would ever say out loud to either of her sisters-in-law.

Josh's current job is dumb and boring, finance adjacent, but he gets up every morning and she makes breakfast and he kisses her and kisses the children. He likes the feel of it, she thinks, the slipping of the suit over his shoulders, the early-morning shower while she makes the lunches for the kids. He maybe hoped he would be more successful, but his parents' money made it easy for him to pretend. Except that money's almost gone now. The steady comfort that so attracted Kate to Josh in college feels far away and separate from the man that he now is.

He yells sometimes, now, after she gets home from the store or if a lot of packages from Amazon show up at once. *The money is not endless, Kate,* he says, in this way that makes her chest get tight, her jaw fix.

She knows she'll hurt Josh, make him feel shame, if she tells her brothers about his botched investments, but she's never wanted a thing in life quite the way she wants to raise her children in the house where her mother raised her. He's not, so far, offered any other options, and she's pretty sure she'll let her husband feel some shame if it might help her get this thing she wants so much.

Alice has laid out old rugs, bright reds and blues, in stretches of the hallway. The floor beneath is dark wood and creaks. The rugs are vacuumed, but not the corners or the baseboards, crumbs stick to Kate's wool socks as she walks through the upstairs rooms. The mess is comfort as much as it's a bother, proof that there are things that she does better than them.

In the room Tess and Martin are sharing with their own kids, Kate runs her hands over Tess's still-closed bag. Her fingers linger on the zipper. She picks up Stella's stuffed platypus and breathes in the scent of kid.

She stands a long time at the entrance to Alice and Henry's bedroom. Their bed is made. The door was open. She thinks of what excuse she might give, were one of them to find her thumbing through their dresser drawers.

"Spying?"

Kate startles, gasps, then laughs. "I wanted to make sure I had a place to hide in case your wife attacked."

Martin grins and holds her shoulder. "You know she's mostly harmless."

"They're kids," she says. "They're just being kids."

She knows Tess is downstairs, angry, that she sent Martin up here to check in—Martin, the same guy who got kicked off the soccer team his senior year for fighting after his teammate cornered freshman Kate and called her chubby.

"She's *anxious*," he says.

She walks from the entrance to Henry's room and leans against the door to one of the hall closets. "Not the word I'd use."

Tess doesn't like Kate's children because they remind Tess too much of all the ways her kids are also flawed. Tess doted on Kate's kids when Helen was still living, but now she refuses to leave them alone with her kids for too long.

Kate's Jack has ADHD, and so does Colin. Kate has not taken Jack to doctors but she assumes. Tess is a lawyer; they have a full-time nanny; she's taken Colin to doctors—the best doctors—

and had it confirmed. Neither can sit still, and they're impulsive. When Jack was small he bit everyone who upset him at pre-school. Late at night sometimes, in bed, her phone underneath the covers, Kate googles how she might better help him. She likes the websites best that say that this will pass.

"Should we give them all a bath?" asks Martin.

Kate looks at her big brother. He's still wearing one of Henry's aprons. She nods toward it. "Mom would be so proud."

Martin puffs his chest out. He's not the type to be embarrassed. Neither of her brothers is. They were kings in high school, tall and handsome, while Kate was doughy, awkward, no one quite believing that she was what came after them.

Martin flattens out the apron. "Nice, huh?" he says. He does not acknowledge Kate's mention of their mother.

"Bea takes showers now," Kate says, annoyed.

"Still. The boys and Stell? So after we eat they can get right to bed."

Tess doesn't let her kids go to sleep without bathing, ever. As if somehow they'll be damaged if the *ritual* the internet says one should deploy at bedtime is disturbed.

Colin is the oldest. Bea's seven to his eight, thirteen months younger. Kate had struggled with nursing, and Helen brought Tess down one weekend with Colin to help. Tess had nursed Bea, shown Kate how to latch her, how to hold Bea in the crook of her arm without feeling afraid she'd break. The ease with which she'd done it had shocked Kate, who always thought she'd be the better mother. But then there was Bea, happy, better satiated by Kate's uptight, too-thin sister-in-law than she'd ever been by her.

"I can do it," Kate says, about the bathing.

"I'll help," Martin says.

She knows Tess told him to stay with her, but she doesn't mind being alone with her big brother. She lived with him off and on in New York her first few years out of school. Their dad had died when Kate was a college freshman, and Martin had come to help her pack her things and drive her home. He was Good, her brother, smart and kind, the sort of person who helped her move apartments, served as guarantor those years their mother couldn't, who didn't call or text too often but who showed up when he needed to show up.

She wants to say now: she wishes that they talked more. She wants to lay her problems out before him—the house, the money—let him make all of it better. She wants to ask him if he knows what to do now that their mother's gone.

"You find the towels," he says, and Kate nods and says nothing. "I'll go track the little monsters down."

Tess sets the table, trying not to listen to make sure Colin isn't misbehaving. She fills a water pitcher and adds ice and thinks briefly of Helen, all the ways this house is so much less than what hers always was. Tess loved Helen more than she'd ever loved a person not her husband or her children. She was sad when she died, but the loss had not felt like hers to mourn. Martin and his siblings had unraveled. The kids too. Helen was seventy-two and had lived a good long life, and Tess felt like it was her job to say this—to Martin and the children on the flight to Florida, to Kate, fetal, on Helen's bed, looking so sad and alone. For years, they'd fought with her to move up to be closer to them—*The whole state is sinking*, said Henry; *What if there's an emergency*, Tess said; *Don't you want to be closer to us*, said Kate—and Helen would look at all of them as if they were five years old, in need of scolding. *If there's an emergency I'll get on a plane,* she said. *And if you want to see me you can come.*

(*Don't tell me about sinking,* she said to Henry. *I'll be long dead before this place goes down.*)

She'd lived her whole life in the state and would not survive, she said, a single winter elsewhere. She couldn't afford the city, couldn't leave the garden she'd spent years building in her yard. *The beauty,* she said, as if it were something tangible she was desperate to keep hold of, as if it lived only there, in her house, in that small stretch of land close to the ocean with the big banyan, backed straight up to acres of federal preserve, and nowhere else. But then she'd had a stroke, quick and sudden, unexpected, and no one had been able to get to her. None of them had seen her in those last hours before she died.

There was no will, a fact for which Tess felt personally responsible. She's a lawyer, should have made sure she had these things in order. How could she have known?

In Florida, as they'd driven back to the airport, after Tess had initiated both the rental and the transfer of the deed of the house, she had thought but hadn't said to Martin that maybe they were losing not just Helen but this whole state that she had come to love, even as they'd all disparaged it all these years: the flatness and the scrub trees; the lushness still for stretches; coco plums, hydrangeas, azaleas, allamandas, bougainvilleas—none of which Tess would have known to name before Helen was hers; the long blocks of concrete pastels on U.S. 1; the way the heat felt wet but also not as bad as it did in New York because they had the sea breeze; the trips to the beach always, after dinner, everybody up late swimming, the water almost always warm; the way the salt stuck to her skin. All those years telling Helen to just let it go, to come be with them, and then Tess feeling, too, like she wasn't ready: how strange it was, to think of a place she'd never been for more than a few weeks as a thing that she had lost.

Grief was new to Tess, still foreign. She knew what it was to live with lack—had built a whole life knowing well enough not to depend on other people—but she hadn't ever lost someone who'd given her so much. Sometimes on the train, a run, walking to the apartment, she gets teary, thinking about Helen, about whatever she might have said when next she left a message on Tess's phone. Just as likely about politics as palaver about a plant that she was growing, just as likely that she had talked to Martin and thought Colin needed to change teachers, thought maybe she could help. She thinks of all those times Helen had flown up to New York for a few days, putting the ticket on a credit card that often, later, Tess and Martin would pay off: taking the children for a few hours on the weekend, baking with them, making all the dinners, Tess relieved and easy on the couch.

She realizes now that living with lack does not prepare you for loss. Lack is an amorphous murk, difficult, unpleasant, but loss weighs more, has a shape and texture all its own.

She knows she should be nice to Kate, who loved Helen more than anybody, who talked to her every day. Tess thinks now that she needs to talk to Kate, to help her, but she feels so much less capable now that Helen isn't here.

• • •

There's no tablecloth for tonight's dinner, which, Tess knows, Helen would have hated. (For Christmas dinner, Kate will have one that she saved from Helen's house.) Henry's in the kitchen, and when Henry cooks, Kate stays away because they're both too possessive in the kitchen. Henry's *too adventurous* in his cooking, Kate says, which Tess thinks means he makes too much of a mess. He only cooks food that was grown or raised within a few miles of where they live, which he's been doing for years but wasn't as easy in the city. Martin still jokes that they only moved so Henry wouldn't starve. He has a greenhouse attached to his studio where they grow plants year-round and he's friends with a handful of local farmers from whom they now get their beef and pork; he'd long been a vegetarian before he and Alice started trying to get pregnant. Those years, he ate everything that Alice told him—chicken livers and ashwagandha, *Tribulus terrestris* for sperm motility—but then the getting pregnant was not the part they'd struggled with.

But the night after tomorrow night is Christmas Eve, and Kate will cook and Henry will follow her instructions. All the siblings used to cook together, fighting, laughing, but following Helen's instructions, standing ready in the kitchen, taking Helen's orders, while Tess and Alice hung out with the kids alone. None of them seems sure how to proceed now.

Alice smokes a fresh cigarette and watches Josh from the corner of the house, careful to stay out of his sight line. There is something calming, solid, about the repetition, the doggedness with which he piles up brick after brick. He was out here within the first half hour of their arrival. He hugged her and Henry, sipped half a drink, roughhoused with the children, got them riled up, and then he walked outside and left Kate to deal with all those sad old boxes of ornaments they brought.

Alice doesn't hate Josh the way Tess does. He's a dilettante, is what Henry says, which is not wrong but also suggests more sophistication than Josh has. He's a know-it-all and he gets obsessed with these useless things that don't make sense. Alice prefers, though, his earnestness to the pretensions of most of her old friends from grad school, who also, mostly, were people obsessed with useless things that didn't make sense. At least Josh's only goal in this igloo endeavor seems to be to please the children. That he's misguided and the kids likely won't notice feels beside the point; at least he's trying, at least this venture, unlike so many of his others, has something vaguely to do with parenting.

"Can I bum one?"

It's Martin, whom Alice likes best when he's not with Tess.

She pulls her pack from her back pocket. "I'll deny it if you're caught."

He laughs. "Quiet out here," he says, handing back her pack and using the end of her cigarette to light his.

"It's creepy," she says. "I wake up sometimes in a cold sweat." Even all those years wandering out there by herself, nature has never felt natural or calming to Alice. What feels natural is walking to the bodega at ten at night to get ice cream or beer, the subway, art, museums, friends and food, miles of sidewalks. All this quiet is so much more ominous than any crowd.

He takes a long drag, and she watches. "Been a while?" she says.

"Too long." They watch Josh pat a block of snow and then another. "Bears?" he says. "Keeping you up?"

"More how ineffectual and destructive humans are," she says.

She feels Martin turn to look at her but does not look back at him. "Ignore me," she says and takes a drag. She looks past Josh to the barn. All the lights are off. Henry is still inside, just as she asked.

"How long you think before Kate tells us she wants the house for herself?"

Alice pulls hard on her cigarette, eyes still on the barn. When she speaks, it sounds apologetic, but to whom, for what, she isn't sure: "Henry has some plan to give it to the birds."

"I love my brother, but you know he's never really had a grown-up thought."

Somewhere inside, right now, Henry's helping with the children. "He's well-intentioned, you know," she says.

"Isn't there a saying about the uselessness of that?"

Alice doesn't take the bait. "You think Tess would go for giving it to Kate?"

Martin's shoulders slump. "I think Tess is very committed to concepts of fair."

"I just don't want to fight about it." Alice grew up in a mostly silent household. She didn't love it, but also, confrontation of most any kind has always made her want to run away.

"I don't imagine," Martin says, watching Josh lean over, pack the snow with both hands, huff, "you or I will be the ones who fight."

Alice clutches her phone in her pocket with her free hand, hoping for a text from Maddie, a moment of uncomplicated interaction, but the phone's inert, unmoved.

"You like the new job?" says Martin, changing the subject. He takes another, slower drag.

It's been almost two years, but Alice doesn't say this. The

move, the shift, it all still feels strangely temporary, like they could live here the rest of their lives and it would still feel like a thing they're trying out. It was sudden and vaguely violent when it happened: this house she got upon the death of her mother's mother, New York forever unsustainable, Alice less interested than ever in the connection making, network building, that they'd moved there for.

"I like the kids," she says, thinking again, briefly, about Maddie.

Martin takes another drag and blows the smoke out the side of his mouth. "Why is everything in life that's pleasurable something that we're not supposed to have?"

"Things are good with you, then?" she says.

Martin laughs. "How long you think Joshy will keep this up?"

"I think your wife might kill him first." Whenever Josh walks into a room, Tess's face gets tight and hard.

"She's mostly harmless," says Martin.

"Kate might not agree with that."

Tess had yelled at Josh their last day in Florida, while they were cleaning out Helen's house, preparing it to be rented. He kept offering advice on what to say to the real estate agent, *useful rental comps* he'd found online. He was officious, always, in everybody's business. *You have to stop it,* Tess said. They were all so sad and tired, ground down after the funeral and the packing and the cleaning. *No one gives a shit,* Tess said. *Just stop.*

For the first time, Helen hadn't been there to make them talk about it after. Helen wasn't there to call each of them over the next few weeks and slowly calm them down. Instead no one talked about it. Kate had looked sad and surprised, and Tess had walked out back to the yard to take a breath; the next day they all left.

"You guys okay up here, though?" Martin says.

He's nicer than Alice lets herself remember. She likes how he seems just slightly more grown-up than Henry. "Your brother is," she says.

He lingers on his cigarette and waits for her.

"It's been a rough few years."

Alice lost five pregnancies in their three years of trying to have a baby, the last one, two years almost to the day of right now, at eleven weeks, the furthest along she'd ever gotten. After that she stayed in bed for a month and hardly spoke to anyone. She'd needed surgery, not once but twice, that last time. They'd just left Brooklyn, and Henry asked Tess to come—Helen was desperate to fly up, but Henry held her off. Tess took the train and then the bus, brought a bottle of gin and six of the tiny chocolate cakes from Alice's favorite coffee shop in the East Village, and sat with her. They drank, and Tess told stories about her most absurd clients, drew her baths and cleaned the house and helped Henry fend off Alice's mom. Tess isn't great at fun, but she's perfect if you need someone to be sad or anxious with.

"Tell me about the kids," her brother-in-law says.

She thinks, at first, he means the babies—though Alice does not believe a fetus is a baby. But she does think it's a collection of cells that portends a whole world of new potentials, both for the carrier and for what the cells might be. She'd thought that fifth time that she'd become inured to hoping, that she wouldn't feel it as sharply. But something in her shifted when they lost it. She had never been a woman who believed one had to be a mother and she did not believe she'd live an empty, barren life now that she wouldn't ever be a mother. But she did know that she would miss the children she would never have, the possibility of them that she'd felt forming, for all the years to come.

"They're amazing," she says, thinking once again of Maddie. Alice collects small things to give her, trinkets near the checkout at the grocery store; Maddie is obsessed with space and animals, and whenever Alice sees a magnet or a figurine she buys it almost without thinking. She's embarrassed, often, to give them to Maddie in front of Quinn; half of them are still hidden in one of her closet drawers. She texts with Maddie, on Henry's phone that Alice gave her—though it's technically forbidden, communicating directly with the children she's in charge of. She works for a nonprofit meant to help families hoping to keep their children, and though there are lots of rules about how employees are meant to interact with the families that they work with, there's hardly any oversight at all.

Quinn pulls the curtains shut as she makes dinner. The streets were empty on their walk back from the Food Town. *She's an anxious person,* says her court-appointed therapist. *Surrender is a necessary and important part of learning to live free of substances.*

Their place is set deep in the ground. You have to walk downstairs after coming in the door, and the windows are all small and blocked, in part, by snow. Their complex is filled with cops, all men, and old women who sit out on their stoops for hours and scowl and smoke. They've all seen her social worker knocking on their door, and they know what it is to have an open CPS case. Quinn knows, if they so chose, her neighbors could report whatever misdeed they might perceive and so, though she wishes they could get more light, she mostly keeps the curtains closed.

She lets Maddie pick the movie, hoping that it's not a documentary. "What's *Free Willy*?" Maddie calls.

"Perfect choice," Quinn says. She drains the pasta, cuts a large lump of butter and stirs it in, sprinkles half a tub of Parmesan on top. "Water?"

"Yes, please."

"Carrots or peppers?"

"Carrots."

When Quinn was separated from her, when she was in the hospital and then in the halfway house, getting counseled, flattened and dulled by the methadone they gave her, her chest like someone had dug a hole inside it, Maddie had learned to cook a few basic meals at the foster home. It was a safe and clean and loving foster home, said Maddie's social worker, but Maddie still won't talk about it a year after coming home. Quinn doesn't like to let her cook now. She likes performing the role of mother, itemizing, sometimes, once Maddie is in bed, all the things she's done that day that prove she's capable and competent.

Quinn cuts off the carrot tops and slices. Maddie queues the movie as she waits for Quinn to set their meals in front of them.

"I cried so hard the first time I watched this movie," Quinn says, passing Maddie her fork and paper towel.

Maddie sidles forward to reach her feet onto the ground, a pillow still between her and her mother, their pasta on their laps.

"You can squeeze my leg," Maddie says. "If you get sad."

Maddie's not the sort of kid to sit close to Quinn while she's awake, and Quinn is grateful, as her daughter tears up watching Willy, that she curls in close. She gets to smell her hair, fresh from the shower, to settle her own body into her daughter's heft and warmth.

"Are we orphans?" Maddie asks her.

"What do you mean, 'orphans'? I'm your mom."

"Yeah, but other people have so many other people. Jason Cretara said they're having twenty-seven people over for Christmas dinner."

"Jason who hit you in the face with the dodgeball last year?"

"Yeah. He's not even nice, and he has twenty-seven people who want to come to his house."

"Sounds stressful and exhausting."

"But who are *our* people? Where are they? Why don't any of them want to have dinner with us?"

Quinn feels queasy. Her skin itches. This isn't the first time Maddie's asked about her family, but she's gotten more unrelenting this past year. "You know we lived with my mom when you were little."

Quinn has not spoken to her mother in three years. She looks at her Facebook almost daily—she had to block her from her own account, but she can log in to her mother's account. The password is Maddie's name and birthday.

Quinn's mother caught Quinn using, while she and Maddie were living with her in the northern Michigan town where Quinn grew up. She said she would have Maddie taken from Quinn if she didn't stop. Quinn wanted to stop. She thought maybe if she moved away she could start over. She thought, also, if she ended up needing to use again, she couldn't risk her mother finding out. She drove up through Canada and back down into New York, Maddie crying, getting carsick. She couldn't afford the city but liked the idea of being close to it. She'd had two grand in savings and took another three grand from her mother. Eventually, she'd sold the car for cash. She liked the quiet and the blankness of the town she found, hoped that there, maybe—separate, different, with none of the people she knew to call for drugs—she might be anything at all.

Of course, she'd eventually found ways to use here, but she's clean now. Lonely but clean; the only friends she'd made these years were the friends that she'd used with.

"But she doesn't even call," says Maddie, still talking about Quinn's mother. "Did she not like me?"

"How could anyone not like you?"

"Then why doesn't she come now?"

Quinn looks at Maddie, picks up both their dishes. She thinks of every awful thing she'd do to protect Maddie, to get to keep her, thinks of her mother's face, all the shitty, angry things she said the day she caught her, thinks of using her mom's phone while she went into another room with Maddie to transfer her mom's savings to herself: "Because she's not nice," Quinn says, sharper than she meant it.

Maddie looks down at her feet.

3

"What can I do?" Alice says to Henry, fresh from the cold and her two cigarettes: emboldened.

"Quit smoking," he says.

"Besides that."

"Wash your hands and cut the pork in thin slices for the tacos."

"You made tacos?"

"For the kids."

She walks up to him and stands on tiptoe, kisses his cheek.

"You like tacos, huh?" he says.

For the first time in a long time she wants to sit here with him. She can't quite conjure the last time they had sex. For so long after she lost the final baby, she didn't want to remember that she had a body. She stopped eating, stopped doing yoga, stopped drinking coffee. Nearly anything that used to please her, she had no interest in. She felt herself wither and liked the feeling, liked the way she felt emptied out.

It was her job that saved her, that latent degree she'd agreed to get so long ago *in case*. Her double major, art and social work. She'd had to take a test to get certified as a therapist but she was good at tests. There was a dearth, she found out as they started researching moving up here, of social workers in rural areas of high need. She went to conferences on opioid abuse and child and family court. She read and learned about all the various broken systems that she'd railed against for years in the abstract. She was pregnant for the last time during all this, and her brain felt sharp and strong, before it dipped into the fog that came with that last loss.

Even after, it had felt good, relieving, to dive so wholly into something concrete and certain, the first real job she'd ever had that she had to go to every day. She'd tended bar through college, and she and Henry had done various art-delivery and -storage gigs to stay afloat in New York. There was other money: from her grandparents and parents, in lump sums, when things got hard. But this: co-workers and a room where there were often bagels or donuts, the bad coffee, the vague way everyone knew at least one thing about everyone else's home life. It was so simple and it saved her. She had to get up every morning, shower. She had to make a joke about the coffee or the donuts so the client she sat across from felt less scared. She was the only Black person in the office; it felt often like she might be the only Black person in their whole small town. This was both familiar to her—she'd been brought up mostly in white spaces—and differently strange. Her clients were angry, often. They had lost their children or their children had lost children. Sometimes they asked if they could have another, different social worker; sometimes they called her awful names. But also, she felt useful. She met with mothers desperate to keep their children, helped them try to work within the systems that seemed built to keep them separated. The texture of her own loss shifted. Here were real live people, structures, inadequacies and failures that had nothing to do with her own body and against which Alice might rail instead.

There were children, also. Every day, Alice got to be with children: a baby on her lap, pudgy, perfect wrists and thighs and small fists she got to hold in her hands; tiny, tentative voices asking her for the snacks she kept stored in her bag; there were bodies, warm and forming, needing, wanting, and though every one reminded her of those five bunches of cells that she'd had briefly but didn't any longer, they also filled up some of all the gaping space that those five bursts of potential left behind.

There was Maddie: a joke on her phone about bananas. A texted fact about chinchillas, a video of just born peregrine falcons, a quiet conversation in her room about black holes.

Tess is the only sober grown-up. It's a family thing, Tess thinks, the way they're all pretending they're not drunk. Josh is sober but he's gone up to shower after his hard work outside. And besides, Josh is not grown-up.

The dining room is straight off the kitchen, separated from the living room by half a wall. Tess sits a minute in the quiet before the chaos, sends a couple work emails on her phone. The table's long, salvaged wood that Henry's sanded down, benches on either side and two large, old, cushioned wrought iron chairs at the ends.

Alice and Henry bring out the tacos, and the kids bound down from upstairs.

Tess calls Stell and Colin to sit close to her. She serves them both and is then embarrassed as Kate's kids all serve themselves. They seem so competent and capable, even as Kate sneaks upstairs to check on Josh. It's not like Tess doesn't know she's too controlling. *From years of familial insecurity,* said the therapist whom she fired not long after he said this. But also, being self-aware has never done much for her besides make her that much better at hating herself.

"You guys have fun?" Henry asks the children.

"Yeah," says Colin, smiling at him.

"What'd you play?" Tess asks.

"Guns," says Stella.

Tess stiffens.

"Sounds fun," Henry says, making himself a fourth taco.

"What do you mean, 'guns'?" says Tess.

"We shot each other," Bea says.

"We all died," says Jack.

Tess gets up to get a can of seltzer from the kitchen before she says something she'll have to apologize for later. Her phone buzzes in her pocket; it's Martin, who is in the other room, at the other end of the table next to Stella.

Only forty-six more hours.

"Josh?" Kate calls. Downstairs they're all talking. She hopes that Tess is finally drunk. "There won't be any food left," she adds.

He wears a sweater and jeans and smells like shower. She likes him less around her brothers. When they're alone together, at home, she likes the way he talks. But when they're anywhere where her brothers and their wives are able to judge him, she can hear every naive thing he says, and it grates.

He was kind to her when they met in college—it was the se-mester after her dad died, and she was still so sad—and that kindness seemed like a good enough reason to be with him. She liked his commitment to grand gestures, a trip to Jamaica their first year together (*Tacky,* said Helen, but she had always been a snob), nice dinners and real dates when most of her friends just had pizza in their dorm rooms, the way he was with her when they were first together, wanting only to be there with her and nothing else. She envied how sure he was all the time, how easy he seemed to expect life to be. She learned later that most of this came from knowing he'd always have money—the comfort that that gave him, the way it protected him from ever having to find out all the ways he wasn't what he thought.

"They couldn't wait?" he says, on the bed now, pulling on his socks.

"*Bedtime,*" she says, mimicking Tess.

"Right," he says.

"You have fun out there?"

"The cold is invigorating." He stands up and pulls her to him. "You hanging in?"

They still have sex a few times a week, and she mostly doesn't mind it, even likes it. The twins were five weeks premature, and from the ages of six months to three years they had weekly two-hour Early Intervention therapy with their therapist, Melanie, who was not much younger than Kate. Melanie never talked about herself, was tall and solidly built, big-eyed with jaggedly cut bangs; she often wore too-big jeans, the bottoms of which would scrape along Kate's hardwood floors. She had been tender with Kate's boys in such a shocking and specific way, and Kate still pictures her sometimes, as she reaches inside herself with Josh inside her too, and always comes more easily. She appreciates the way that what her husband wants, when they have sex, is something she can give him, the way that after, he goes right to sleep.

She often brings her computer into bed after he's passed out and watches hours of baking shows until the sun's up; she doesn't mind that much how tired she is the next day; it's such a treat to have that space of time in which no one talks and no one's touching her.

"You get your picture?" asks her husband.

It's a thing Helen would do, the outfits, except now she's not here. Kate knows Tess thinks she's ridiculous and will get the children ready muttering the whole time about how silly Kate is. She won't help her keep the kids entertained or tell them to smile or fix Colin's bow tie. She won't offer to reimburse her for Stella's dress. Three days from now, with some snarky comment below it but still not giving Kate credit, Tess will post the perfect picture Kate took while Tess was refilling her drink in the kitchen and she'll get a thousand likes, a thousand comments about her gorgeous perfect family.

"Not till Christmas," she says.

"Of course," says Josh.

His hand lingers on her waist, and he kisses her. She wants not to think, to like him again, to be reminded of the weight and heft of him such that the quality, the small ways he is not what she hoped he would be, feels less like the point. She slips her tongue into his mouth. He cups her ass, and she leads him into the room where Alice has piled towels for all of them on the bed, Josh's still in a crumple on the floor. He sidles her up onto the old dresser in the corner of the room and it rocks and she gets nervous, looking toward the unlocked door. She grabs his shoulder, his pants now around his ankles, sweater still on. Her one pant leg is off, the other hanging from her foot. His free hand, big and rough but gentle nonetheless, is cupped over her mouth and, for a second, there is a sound outside the door; they both freeze and his hand gets tighter on her mouth and she bites down, breathing through her nose; he winces; once they've waited long enough to know that whatever the sound was, it's far from them, he releases himself into her, and there's a thunk as he makes one final thrust and they both freeze and stare back at the door.

He keeps his hand on her waist and kisses her, her back cold against the mirror. Her ass hurts. He pulls his pants back up and smiles. She catches sight of herself briefly in the mirror and winces at the smush of breasts and belly, grabs for her clothes. Josh looks triumphant as he buttons up his shirt. "Should we go wrench some food from the vultures?" he says.

She stands a minute, her hair mussed, skin splotched, touching her fingers to her cheeks in front of the mirror. She pulls up the waist of her jeans, breathes in, pulls her shirt down long over her ass. She's grateful that Henry and Alice mostly fill their walls with art and not with family pictures. She's grateful that, mostly, she can avoid catching sight of Helen's face. But on the dresser, right next to where she just fucked her husband, she sees a photo of her mom at Martin's wedding, so much younger, smiling, arms wrapped around Kate's brothers. Helen is so completely Helen: her hair, her smile, the way her hands hold so tightly to her sons' waists.

She hears Josh call to Henry about a creak he found on the banister as he heads downstairs, and she looks again at her mother, then back at herself in the mirror, then away. Fingers hard against her face, palms pressing into each of her cheeks, Kate breathes in and holds the air a second in her belly—thinking of the yoga that she sometimes does on YouTube while the kids are at school—then breathes out long through open lips.

Alice goes to get more drinks in the kitchen, to start to clear the plates from the kids who have run back upstairs, having cleaned their hands and faces—having said they did. She gets a text from Maddie and responds too quickly. She's had her phone with her all night in case. Maddie doesn't text her every day but she does often. Sometimes three or four times quickly, especially this time of night. Maddie sends long paragraphs about what she's reading, sometimes GIFs or long strings of emojis. She asks Alice how she is, and Alice is never sure the right way to respond. Hi, says this one, followed by a smiley-face emoji. Hope you're having a good night. Now, Alice sends her another picture of the Christmas tree, all decorated. As she sends it, she marvels at how beautiful it is, how she and Henry would never have decorated a tree themselves, maybe not even gone to get it. But she likes the feel of it when she comes down the stairs.

She adds a second text: Send yours?

She and Henry had gone to cut the tree in the woods close to their house, one of the few times in the past year they've spent more than a couple of hours together. *We have to take advantage,* Henry had said. *Upstate living.* It was a joke they often made, the two of them, when it snowed for days on end or someone made some racist comment to Alice at the grocery store. This time, though, he meant it differently. He'd been trying, the past month or two, to make her smile. He tried to talk to her about his work out in the barn, his flock of birds, about her clients, about the children, politics and weather. Far too often, Alice shut him down.

Once, a few weeks before they got the tree, before the snow started in earnest, Henry made them breakfast, and they ate together, and as soon as he started to try to ask her questions she got quiet and cold and got scared she might start to cry or yell, and he went outside to work. When the door shut as he headed out back, she got in the car, not acknowledging that she knew where she was going, and drove to Maddie and Quinn's. She was allowed—required, in fact—to show up unannounced to check up on them.

She'd knocked on the door that day in jeans and Henry's old hooded Bowdoin sweatshirt, her hair pulled back. Quinn was watching TV, Maddie reading. The condo was small and dark, the windows made more narrow by the portion of the place that was built into the ground. It felt warm, though, safe and settled, extra held together. The way the living room was separated from the kitchen with an unnecessarily large wall. Quinn made her a perfect cup of French press coffee. Maddie told her about her book, a princess running away to live with dragons. There was a small, round table in the corner of the kitchen but only two stools, so they'd all sat on the couch, TV still on and none of them talking. Alice had felt better being with them, the sound of Maddie breathing close to her.

"Time for bed, kid," Quinn says.

Maddie is already half-asleep next to her, the phone the social worker gave her still clutched in her hand. Quinn sets the phone down on the couch and lifts her. Maddie hardly lets her do this any longer, and Quinn is grateful, holding her like this. She wants to tell her that she's sorry that their family is so small, but also, more people mostly means more awful and exhausting obligations; mostly Quinn's relieved that it's just them.

"I have to brush my teeth," says Maddie as Quinn carries her past the bathroom.

"Of course." Quinn sets her down and spreads the toothpaste on her daughter's toothbrush and her own. They both brush, and Quinn makes a face at her with the toothpaste's foam around her mouth, and they both laugh.

Maddie changes out of her clothes and into her pajamas, and Quinn settles her in with the stuffed peregrine falcon that the social worker found for her.

"Read to me?" says Maddie. She's mostly read herself to sleep since she was four.

"A treat!" Quinn says, picking up the book on Maddie's nightstand and opening to the page she's folded over.

"Lie down with me?" says Maddie.

"Of course." Quinn pulls back the blanket and settles in next to her daughter. "Close your eyes, my girl."

Quinn slips out of Maddie's bed and back into the living room, flipping through the channels on low volume, scrolling through her phone. She hates this time: Maddie fast asleep and so much night left. She thinks of walking to the Hudson, or going back into Maddie's room to watch her sleep. She scrolls slowly through her mother's mostly dormant Facebook page. Mary posts pictures of the sky sometimes, of her and her friend Susan, at a church function three weeks ago, all dressed up. Quinn checks her ex-boyfriend's Instagram. He was the first boyfriend she'd had since she got Maddie back. He yelled at her sometimes when she made him angry, his face close to her face and his words loud and hard. Quinn had liked the weight of him next to her at night when she came home from work and after Maddie was in bed. Not enough, though, not more than she liked Maddie talking during dinner, not more than she liked having her daughter mostly to herself. Still, the quiet, this time of night, makes her feel crazy; the urge to get free of her own skin is hard to fight.

When she first got the Oxys—after she had Maddie, by C-section, drugs that made her teeth chatter—they told her to *stay ahead of the pain.* She was a child, seventeen, and maybe no one cared she was so young now that she was a mother. Maddie's father was a rich kid, Quinn's age, in town with family friends from Chicago for the summer; Mary had screamed and yelled at the mention of an abortion, even as she'd spent all those years saying what an awful drain having Quinn had been on her. The pills were the closest Quinn could get to breathing, sitting quiet and a little less afraid. They were expensive, though, and she'd just moved out of her mother's house for the first time; she had a job waiting tables that gave her three weeks' leave. Her mother was a town away but too busy to help. She came over one or two nights the months that Quinn was about to not make rent and needed to pick up an extra shift.

Eventually, Quinn put Maddie in day care and took mostly day shifts, which meant less money. Maddie was so small still, squirming, chirping, not yet rolling over. Quinn felt sad and afraid each time she passed Maddie off to the klatch of women who cared for her while Quinn worked, who offered only formulaic summaries of when Maddie napped, how many bottles she'd been fed. The day care, too, cost too much. Maddie was still waking up a few times a night, needing to be walked back and forth from the kitchen to the bed, sleeping only when she was settled in against Quinn's skin. Quinn was exhausted, broke, and worried. A friend at work suggested heroin, because, she told her, it was the least expensive way this friend had found to get a break. This friend turned out, unsurprisingly, to be fucking the guy who sold Quinn her first hit of heroin, but by the time Quinn found that out she'd already felt the warm and quiet rush of it, and the woman hadn't lied about how cheap it was.

Still, Quinn only ever shot up to stay steady. She was a good and present mother. She rejected the idea that one could not be lots of things at the same time. Her own mother had never touched a drug in her life, went to church on Sundays, didn't drink or smoke. She was all those things and also—Quinn hadn't lied to Maddie— she wasn't very nice. She cleaned houses for rich people; she cleaned the houses of all the people who came to town in summer, who hired Quinn's mom to stock their fridges in advance, to empty out their houses once they'd gone back to their lives.

When she was younger, Quinn had often gotten strange, shapeless aches up on her forehead, in her belly; she felt dizzy sometimes for no reason, and the school would call her mother. Her mom would yell the whole way home about how the money didn't come by magic, that she had to work to make it, that she could not fucking believe that she could not ever, not since the day Quinn was born, get a fucking break.

She could be kind, too, Quinn's mom. She could be fun, used to tell bad jokes to make Quinn laugh. Sometimes the memes she shares on her Facebook page still make Quinn laugh. Quinn thought often, after she had Maddie, that maybe there simply had not been space or time or energy left over for her mother to be good to her, to be nice, more often than she was.

• • •

Right now, in a drawer inside a drawer inside the closet in Quinn's room—you have to reach up to know it's there, a thin slat of flat wood with a green felt bottom—are three pills, tramadol, that Quinn's boyfriend left. Quinn found them in the back pocket of his pants, sealed up in a small bag, very early in the morning, when he was still asleep. She'd known his dad's new girlfriend had had surgery three weeks before and thought, perhaps. She had to not think while she reached her hand into each pocket. She had to not think about the weight and feel of them as she reached for and held them in her hand; she held them separate from her body as she carried them across the room and put them in the drawer.

When he asked her later: asking was admitting that he had them, would out him as not-clean if she didn't have them; was risking, according to the promises she'd made him make when they first met, Quinn telling him that he could not come back. But he was more concerned, it turned out, with getting the pills back than pretending to have kept any of the promises he'd made to Quinn.

"Did you see anything in my pants?" he said to her, too loud. He didn't have his shirt on, though she'd asked him lots of times to have his shirt on when Maddie was awake. He'd gotten up two hours after Maddie, come bounding into the kitchen, his hands deep in his pockets, hair mussed, shoulders leaning forward, body hard. Both she and Maddie had already eaten. Maddie was reading on the couch.

His face came too close to hers, and Quinn tried to angle her eyes past him to make sure Maddie was still far enough away that she couldn't hear. She'd laughed at him. "In your pants?"

she said, letting their eyes meet, smiling but no longer laughing. "What should I have found?"

He stepped back, his head shaking, looking toward the other room where Maddie sat. "Useless bitch," he said.

Hours later, Quinn and Maddie hadn't talked about it. He'd gone back into her room to get his shirt and keys and phone, and he'd walked out, and Maddie hadn't looked up from her book. Quinn had folded laundry, done the dishes, reorganized the stack of books by Maddie's bed onto her shelf. She'd let her stay on the couch all day reading, playing on her phone, instead of forcing her outside. She checked on the pills that day only once. She gave Maddie a plate of salami and sliced cheese for lunch so she could eat it still holding her book. For dinner they ate leftover takeout pizza and watched *Home Alone,* Maddie falling asleep on the couch next to Quinn. When Quinn took her into her room Maddie woke up and looked at her.

"No more useless men," her daughter said.

Sometimes, on these nights when Quinn can't breathe, she thinks of walking the two blocks to the nearby bar to have a single beer to steady herself. She's done it twice, and no one got hurt and everything was fine. She didn't relapse. Maddie was safe and warm in bed when she got home. There was something thrilling, even, after all those days and weeks of doing all the things she knew she was supposed to do—BEING A GOOD MOTHER—to just stop it, to sit quiet and alone and pretend that she was someone else.

Instead Quinn goes in Maddie's room a final time to move the book in her bed to her nightstand, pull her covers over her feet. She gets in bed and pulls up a *Housewives* show on her phone and lets the women yell next to her face until she passes out.

4

Henry opens a beer in the kitchen, anxious. Out the window, he can see the outline of the barn and starts to think of what he'll do once he's free to get to work. Next to him is *The Evolution of Beauty*, an extraordinary book, exhilarating, about the impact and the power of female preference based on beauty, the actual restructuring of the interior of female ducks in order that they retain reproductive agency.

Whenever he's not working, Henry's reading. Sometimes, when Alice thinks he's working, he's next to the woodstove in the barn with one of these books about birds, or about climate, about the inevitable, horrifying devastation that still lies in front of all of them. He prefers the terror that arises from this reading to the amorphous sort of dread that he imagines Martin and Kate, his whole family, with their vaguely unexamined good intentions, their offhanded *burning world* jokes, must walk around with every day. For years, this knowledge made him angry: eleven-mile-long cracks in the ice shelf, carbon trapped inside of sheets of ice that, when released, will turn to methane, heatwaves so extreme that people will die out on the street; tens of

millions of people displaced, Miami, Bangkok, Bangladesh, all
gone; 17 percent less crop yield; unprecedented storms, unprecedented fires, unprecedented droughts; air that isn't breathable;
new and resurgent and more widespread plagues; a hundred
times more species extinct than would have been extinct if not
for human beings; a hundred thousand birds each year dying,
just in New York City—running into buildings, flying into the
sharp glint of high-rise windows, spiraling straight down to the
ground; a 10 to 20 percent increase in the likelihood of armed
conflicts, three, four, more new Syrias a year. For years, he had
compiled and acquired information and then enacted the fury
that he felt about it in his work.

Alice thought he was immune to any sense of whether anybody cared about or bought or paid attention to the things he
made, but really, it had been easy to keep going as long as she was
there. She knew more about form than anyone he'd ever known,
had always been the more ambitious, better at the parties and the
networking and the slide submissions, better at making a career.
He'd trusted her enough—her commitment not only to her own
work but to his—to keep going. Except then she'd stopped making. To see her every day but separate, to go to work without her
there: his anger had shifted, to his own ineffectuality, the uselessness of what he did; the solar panels he'd ordered last winter were
still in the attic. They both drove electric cars, but what help was
that? The change they needed was monumental and systemic.
He should run for office, camp outside the door of his various
congresspeople. Be active. Instead he went out to his barn and
made more birds. He came inside at night and tried to make his
sad wife laugh. The weight of this—everything he wasn't—felt
different without Alice there beside him, knowing what he did.

It felt sharper, more granular and local, after all those years of trying for a baby. He didn't even really want a baby, felt it was destructive, willful ignorance—and yet. He had spent years with no one who seemed to see or feel what he saw or felt, except for Alice, briefly—and then all that stupid hope. And then Alice gone again.

It's well past both kids' bedtimes, and Stella is cranky, languid, clutching her stuffed platypus. Colin's jumping on the bed. Tess is so relieved to be alone with just her husband and her kids. *Her* family, she thinks, and then feels bad for thinking it.

"Stop!" says Martin. The duvet is a jumble, and half the pillows have fallen. Tess is working to get the fitted sheet onto the air mattress Alice has blown up on the floor for Colin and Stell to share.

"Martin," Tess says. They have to get the extra pillows out of the car, and she's worried Stella might complain about the texture of the blankets. She needs all of them to go to sleep so she can breathe a bit, maybe write some work emails, before she gets to sleep herself.

"He has to calm down," says Martin.

"He's—"

"Please don't tell me that he's tired."

"He is. We all are." He thinks she makes too many excuses, is too easy on them, but they *are* tired. They're little kids.

"He needs to control himself," says Martin. He's drunk too much, Tess thinks. Martin gets annoyed with Colin even when he hasn't been drinking. He's on edge, she thinks: this first holiday without his mother, this thing at work. Martin talked on the phone with Helen almost every day. There were weeks and months when Tess worried Helen knew more about her husband's life than Tess. Helen was more patient, had more free time. Tess thinks how strange it is for Martin to be facing his first moment of crisis without her here to call.

"Colin," Martin says, more calmly, grabbing his arm.

"Rrrrroar!" says Colin, snapping at his dad. The sound of his teeth clamping down is loud in Tess's ears.

Martin grabs Colin with both hands and brings his face into their son's face. "You do not bite!" he says, too loud.

"Martin!" Tess says.

"*What* is wrong with you?" Martin says.

"Martin, stop."

He looks at her and steadies himself. He whispers to Colin, "You cannot do that, do you understand?"

Colin looks small and scared, but also, Tess can't be sure what he'll do next, whether he might now lash out again. More than anything about their son, this is what frightens Tess, that at any moment, he might explode; that also, he might crumple; that she can't ever tell how to stop or help in either circumstance.

When she was little, sometimes, when her mother was sad because her father had a woman who was not her to whom he often went after work—Tess's mother would come into Tess's room at night and talk to her. Not often—once a month, maybe twice. Her mother would cry and run her fingers through her daughter's hair, ask Tess to scoot over, curl in next to her. The warmth of Tess's mother's body against Tess's body was a comfort; there was not much touching in her family. Tess didn't think that her mom meant for this to be a comfort to Tess, but it was. Sometime in the weeks leading up to Tess's eleventh birthday, her mom began to bring her tiny blue-and-yellow cosmetics bag into bed with her. She still talked and cried, still said, *Scoot over, Tess-girl,* but also, right before that, she pulled out the same tiny scissors she used to maintain her perfect nails and cut nicks into Tess's feet. Her hand was small and firm and warm on Tess's heel, and blood popped up, and Tess stayed very quiet and very still. Her mom was careful after to stanch the bleeding, to keep the sheets clean. She always cut above the heel, below the ankles so that, even with the shortest socks, the wounds could not be seen. Sometimes, when Tess is tired and angry, when Colin acts like this and she gets scared, she worries over all the ways her mother is inside of her, inside of him; she worries over who and how both she and he might hurt.

Stella's still standing, watching, her shirt off—never as much like the baby that she so recently was as when the perfect pouch of her belly is out in the open. She's meant to be changing into her pajamas but stares, instead, at all three of them. Martin hardly ever notices the ways that Stella can be difficult too, the ways she clings when they're out in public, the way she so quickly feels beat up or down by small slights. Instead, he seems to take every moment when Colin loses control personally, as if it is proof that they have failed at parenting. When, later, they're alone and she reminds him Colin's impulsiveness is not his fault—and Martin does look sad and sorry, chastened, able, even, sometimes, to see that he too lacks control—he still can't quite not be infuriated by the ways their son somehow isn't what he'd hoped.

"Colin," Tess says. "Come here, baby."

Colin hisses one more time but quietly enough they can all pretend they didn't hear him. Martin loosens his grip and Tess watches, her body still, willing her son to walk toward her.

· · ·

Alice takes a long, hot shower now that the house is still and quiet. She turns on the small space heater on her side of the bed, fists both her hands and rolls them along the edges of her hips. Her wrists still clench when she's tense, although she used to blame the painting, the ripping canvas, *working*. She misses having somewhere to put all the extra anxious, worn-out self that she still has. Her work now is more solid, like those years trying to have a baby had felt at first. It has clear, concrete goals, clear, concrete steps: the meetings, the court hearings, the pro- tocols, and the people, just like the special foods, the yoga, the long walks; lying on the bed and visualizing the healthy, forming fetus, hands flat on her stomach, deep breaths in for a count of six, out for a count of eight. But art and baby had also begun, that last year, to feel similar: rules that felt specific and exact but also made up; trying to be precise, but precise like jumping off a cliff. Art was from the body, while a baby would be of it; art was mushy, murky, abstract, while a baby would be solid—the obses- sion and compulsion were exactly like she'd always done them, but then all that time and work for nothing. In that way, too, it felt like art.

She's most grateful for her job now because she doesn't have to deal with her own thoughts as often. Sometimes, those years of the failed art and the failed baby (her art was not a failure, Henry said, but no one gave a shit about it, so what else could it have been?)—when she felt empty, awful—she thought of call- ing Helen. She thought of asking Helen to love her, make it better. But what a stupid, silly, childish thing to say, to ask. *I do already,* is what Helen would have said. What Alice wanted was someone to prove it to her, prove something irrevocable about her, say it in such a way that she could feel sure they would not take it back. Helen was the only one she might have trusted. Henry seemed to want her too unthinkingly to see how wanting wasn't loving. With every man who'd ever wanted her and called it love, she'd felt like this. This was true too, in its way, of how her mother loved her. Preconditioned. The baby was something both Henry and her mother wanted that she couldn't give. Henry said he didn't, it was her choice, but she knew better. She thought maybe her body couldn't hold a baby because it understood she'd never really learned to love another person—maybe also this was why her art failed; she'd not been shown or taught enough about just loving without first appealing or performing; this was her body's way of keeping all her future children safe.

And then when she stopped working, and then with her new job and all the ways it shocked her, scared her, made her feel inadequate and helpless too, she'd never picked up the phone and called Helen—not with the art or with the babies, not this past year when her job got murky. It's a particular type of sad, she thinks, to miss the possibility that she might one day call this person who is gone now, that what she lost was a thing she never had the courage to go get.

Josh is out back again, but Kate almost doesn't mind it. It's been dark so long it feels much later than it is. Parenting is easier when she can focus solely on the task at hand. She piles everyone's pajamas on the bed and makes a game of who can get them on quickest while she makes up the bed. She brings Bea over to the desk chair, close to the window, and braids her long hair, as she does every evening so that it doesn't knot in the night. The twins try to sabotage one another and both of them fall over and they yell, but she just lets them be. When Bea's braid is done, she gets up to tickle the twins, and their screams switch to squeals, and Kate finishes the bed then piles in with them and tickles Bea.

"If all three of you behave tomorrow," she says, thinking, again, of Tess, easing them into bed and giving each kid their own blanket, "you can open one present before bed on Christmas Eve."

"Can you sleep with us?" Bea says as they settle.

"There's not room, duck."

"Put Daddy on the floor," Jamie says.

Kate smiles. "I'll lie down with you awhile."

She wishes they were sweet like this always. She loves this time of night, when they're already half-asleep. She pulls out the extra blankets that she found in the hall closet, the extra pillows Josh brought in from the car. Alice gave them an old queen mattress and a twin on the floor, and Kate spreads the blankets and the pillows so it's just one big nest and she settles them all in. She gives Bea a book and reads one to the boys, and they're asleep before she's halfway through it. She brings Bea up into the bed with her and lets her read beside her and somehow, all too quickly, falls asleep.

"Might be a storm tomorrow," Josh says to Henry. He gets himself a beer. He's bright red, skin chapped from the outdoors, and he uses the sleeve of his shirt to wipe the sweat off his face. He sits opposite Henry at the crooked homemade island, beer before him, staring at his phone. "What's your ZIP code again?"

Henry tells him.

"Wintry mix tomorrow night."

"Good thing we have the house," says Henry.

They're both quiet. Josh opens an Audubon book, flips a couple pages.

"You see Panic again this year?" Henry says, trying. Josh's been going to see Widespread Panic at Red Rocks in Colorado every year since before he met Kate. This infuriates Kate, of course. Also Helen and Tess. The shows were usually in summer, and the twins were born in May; Helen had driven from Florida to Richmond so Kate wouldn't be alone with all the kids the year the twins were born. *At least it isn't Phish,* said Alice. *At least it isn't Dave Matthews Band.* But Henry's always respected this about Josh, this particular commitment, a small, sure way he'd pissed off his uptight father—that and his ridiculous long hair.

"Joe and I drove out," Josh says. "Brandt got some big promotion and couldn't come."

"A good time?" Henry says.

"Yeah," Josh says. "Your sister got sort of pissed."

"She's got a lot . . ." starts Henry, wanting to defend her. He used to talk so often to his mother; she told him to check in on his sister, visit Tess when the kids were babies, and he listened, followed her directions: *You must be active in your own life,* Helen said; *you must engage and interact in order to create.* But he's done nothing, really, since she died. He's not sure he knows how without her, to engage or to be helpful. He keeps working, not because of any grand plan or because he thinks anyone will

ever notice, but because of how scared and sad and worthless—
hopeless—he'd feel all day if he stopped.

"How's the work?" Josh says, closing the bird book. "Work" feels
both overly generous and reductive. He can't bring himself to say
"art."

"It's fine," says Henry. "Keeps me busy."

Josh isn't sure how Alice and Henry support themselves. Kate's
mentioned a lump sum from a dead grandma, this house they
got from her. Josh isn't sure, in fact, how almost anybody lives
without windfalls like this. Once, years ago, Josh got in a fight
with Martin, told him it was a travesty to pay more than fifty
dollars for their family's cell phone coverage. Josh had never paid
a phone bill, though, and didn't know that there weren't family
plans for less. He knew that if at any point they'd had to live off
only what he made, a thing that now feels likely, he would not
know how to keep his family safe and fed. It feels grown-up
to know this. It also feels like a secret that he wants to keep to
himself.

"How's yours?" Henry says.

"You know," says Josh. "Busy, I guess."

The truth is that for the fourth time in ten years, the position
just above him came open and his bosses hired from outside instead of offering Josh the promotion. Josh wonders now if always
knowing, generally, that he'd be fine has made it harder for him
to be the sort of person who moves up. He wonders about the
ways his father was *self-made*, how he talked to both Josh and
his brother like they were still children, how their money was attached specifically to an adviser that their father chose, and how

for so long all of this felt like a gift. Now he's old enough to have built something of his own but hasn't. When his father died he felt set free but also not prepared—the first thing he did was fire that adviser, oversaturate his stocks. He sees now that he's never quite learned how to live.

"I input data into spreadsheets," Josh says. "Then I input that data into other spreadsheets that punch out different data that I then put into reports." It's completely pointless, Josh doesn't say but knows now, completely pointless and it doesn't even keep his family fed.

"That's not dissimilar to what I do," says Henry, nodding toward the books in front of him, still open. "I collect data. I take things in, take other things in, and then I put everything that I've collected into something else."

"At least what you do has the possibility of showing something, bringing awareness about something," Josh says. "Not just the same old empty capitalist shit."

"Who do you know that has any interest in art?"

Josh stays quiet.

"And who among them talks about the climate? Who among them is actively trying to not fuck up the world?"

Henry seems angry now, and Josh didn't mean to make him angry. He was trying to get along, to express interest. He was trying, he thinks, to bond.

"I think most people," Josh says. "They're just living. They're just trying to live."

Alice wraps her hair and puts on one of Henry's flannels. She pulls on thin cotton pants and thick wool socks. She keeps a book by her bed, which she opens to start reading. She keeps picking up her phone to see if Maddie's texted back, but she has not.

"Making resolutions?" Martin says to Josh and Henry. They sit up straighter as he walks into the room. Henry seems angry, Josh apologetic.

For years, since Martin's second year in college, they made solstice resolutions on the twenty-first, such a perfect Helen thing. Quantitative as well as qualitative: concrete things they wanted to accomplish, feelings they hoped to have. Kate reminded everybody to start thinking about it via text two weeks before. It's the twenty-second now.

Martin does not feel like making resolutions in the absence of his mother. What's the point, really, without her there to hear? But he does not feel like sleeping, either, especially after yelling at his son. Martin has begun to feel old and tired and he thinks maybe, if Josh leaves, he could tell his brother about this. It has only happened in this past year. It used to be that his job kept him feeling young. It's embarrassing, in fact, the largesse that he's experienced until now. His wife makes gobs of money. He does fine and adds to the equation a sense of seriousness, respectability—a vaunted institution with which to be associated, a sufficiently esoteric set of knowledge points that make him impressive enough at dinners and parties. He loves the rhythm of the classroom, its constant shifts and evolutions, the way an idea stretches, morphs, as students press and question, as he tries to lead them through a text. He brings the best snacks to committee meetings, advises student organizations when he's asked. Summers off are meant for writing papers, but mostly he ignores this. In late May and June, when he has off and the kids are still in school, he lets their nanny take a month of paid vacation, takes the children to and from school and helps with homework, makes the dinners. Colin doesn't have the patience, but Martin's already taught Stella how to cook some basic meals. He used to take the kids to Helen's for a week as soon as school let out. He jokes he is a kept man in summer, except Tess says she doesn't think this joke is funny. The last four weeks they send the kids to the sort of fancy camps they can only afford because of her, and he bangs out just enough—a paper or two that no one will read, an outline for the next one, a proposal for a conference—that he will not be questioned by his department head come fall. He does not, in other words, have ambition like his wife has ambition. His mother loved him too much, is what she says, in a tone not absent accusation. He likes their life just fine as it is, is the not not an accusation he hurls back.

Now, though, his students feel separate. They use language he can't recognize, are wary of him on sight. "White men," they say, "toxic," and they look at him as if, were he a better teacher, he'd have long since become something else. He's a good guy, he wants to tell them. His mother raised him as a feminist. He got up at night with both his children, changed them, walked them up and down the hall of their apartment while Tess slept. He has spent more days alone with them than she has. His wife can be sharp and cold, and still he loves her. He can admit now, though this he would not share with his students, that he likes that she did not know intimacy or love before him.

He's not one of those guys who had to reassess his approach after the first kerfuffle of allegations. After some of his colleagues started to get together to troubleshoot, after some were quietly pushed out. What he's been accused of now, though, is *insensitivity to neurodiversity in the classroom.* What he's been brought up on is a *lack of openness to alternate views.* He built a career on *alternate views,* for fuck's sake. He teaches Hannah Arendt. He teaches José Martí, Benedict Anderson. Societies and communities. He had liked a student, trusted her, treated her too intimately perhaps; he let his guard down, *crossed a boundary,* and he might now lose twenty years of work as a result.

He had googled her sometimes, this girl, on his phone, in bed at home after Tess had gone to sleep. It was not so specific as attraction, the thing he felt toward her. She was attractive, but she also seemed mostly like a child. He wanted to talk to her and to remember what it felt like to be hopeful. He wanted to be able to imagine what life would be, instead of to know so much what it was. He'd watched a video of her playing the guitar on YouTube over and over. Four minutes, twenty-eight seconds. She was in a band, she'd told the class the first day, had made a music video, in which she sat languidly on a windowsill and sang about a kind of loss Martin felt sure she'd never seen up close. She had thick eyebrows, big, dark eyes. Even Martin knew that she was average, really. It was the talking to her that he liked: her gesticulating, the way she seemed so worked up so much of the time.

It was someone else who had accused him. A girl who also had complained about other men on staff. She seemed—and he was not allowed to say this—to have it out for most men she met. He had known since he'd first met her to be afraid of her. She talked too much about herself in class; Martin had not been able to get her to be quiet. What he'd done, what he'd done wrong and why he knew this was all his fault, was talk to this other girl, the YouTube guitar girl, about this problem girl.

It had been during office hours, after an especially hard class. After a class in which the girl would not stop talking about how much her mother didn't understand her, even though the book they'd read, the conversation, had nothing to do with that. *Back to the text,* Martin kept saying, and the girl kept talking. She'd gone on almost ten minutes about her mother's myopia with regard to her relationship to her hair and body, and Martin had wanted to stand up and yell at her to stop. Colin and Stell had both been sick that week, and it was only a few months after they'd lost Helen. And then the girl, the guitar girl, had followed him into his office to ask about the paper they had due. She was diligent and confident, not afraid to address him by his first name, not afraid to tell him when she thought the class conversation wasn't as productive as she'd hoped. She followed him into his office and he sat down and was still worn out by this other girl. He had been so fucking tired. He'd talked shit, is what he would later say to Tess when he tried to explain the whole thing. He'd talked shit about this one child with another, which he was too old and too smart to do, but that's what he had done. He'd called her demanding and exhausting. He'd made a joke at her expense. In the way of students, in the way of children—which is, he remembers now, what all of them are—word had gotten from the guitar girl to the problem girl and the problem girl had, rightfully hurt and upset, reported him.

Letters had been written, documents drawn up. Nothing will come of it, he has been reassured by colleagues, *not concrete enough*—but he feels unmoored, afraid, thinking about stretches of time without the classes and the students and his small, single-windowed office. He has an email draft telling both women that he's sorry, but Tess says he cannot give them written proof.

Tess didn't want to tell his siblings. Martin didn't either, and he was relieved when Tess said as much out loud to him. If Helen were still alive, he would have told her. And then his siblings would have known within the week. And then he'd have someone besides Tess to talk to about it.

Instead, now, no resolutions and no Helen. Just Henry flipping through his bird book and Josh staring at his igloo out the window. Josh asks a question about what Martin's teaching, and Martin pretends he's teaching what he taught last year. How societies can be built, but communities are *felt;* the difficulties of individually constructed, artificially imposed collectivity. No constructed community has any chance of long-term survival until the third generation. Josh asks more things, and Martin gives some opaque answers about theory that he knows Josh won't understand, and Henry smirks, and they move on. Josh brings up the weather again, says it might *get nasty* later, shows Martin and Henry a moving weather system—greens and yellows, spots of orange—on his phone.

Martin watches Henry as a lull falls. He wonders how it is, in all these years, they never learned to talk without their mother. Now there is only all the space and quiet where she should be and is not.

"Should we play cards?" asks Martin, because he can't take the silence. Tess will hate this, but he doesn't want to go to sleep yet.

"Should I go get the girls?" asks Josh.

Martin winces, knowing Tess won't come if Josh asks her, certain Tess will somehow hear that Josh called her a "girl."

"I'll go up," he says, taking his beer.

"I'll get Alice," Henry says.

"It's late," says Tess, just as Martin knew she would. She's on her phone checking work email, and he knows she'll be up for hours still.

"It's nine o'clock."

"I want to get up to run."

"There's too much ice out on the roads."

She reaches next to the bed and holds up a mess of netted metal. "Henry gave me these to put on my shoes."

"You're not going to sleep; you're working," he says.

"No one else at work is on vacation yet."

Martin looks past her, toward the sleeping children.

"Can you ask Henry for the Wi-Fi password?"

"You can ask him when you come downstairs."

She stands up, still holding her computer. "We should talk about the house."

He takes it from her. "We can maybe talk about the house, but your computer stays here."

Tess sits, phone in hand and far enough away, she hopes, to look at email. Kate and Josh are on the couch and close to one another. Martin and Alice and Henry are all cross-legged on the floor with beers.

Tess hates games, but Helen always used to make them play. *We're grown-ups*, Tess often said to Martin before or later, *why must we play games?* But it filled up the time. It was better, certainly, than trying to talk about real things. Six weeks ago, Tess terminated a surprise pregnancy and told no one—a faulty IUD, which, said her gynecologist, was less rare than one might think. Helen had died six months before, but it still felt so close. Tess took a test alone at work. She'd come home the night after the procedure; she'd told her bosses one of the kids was sick because she'd never called in sick herself. She'd gone to bed early, claiming nausea, and felt only a small pang of guilt when Martin had gone out special after feeding the kids dinner to the fancy grocer near their old apartment, to get her her favorite organic ginger ale.

Tess is forty-two and tired. Her kids are kids now, and she is grateful for it. They are potty trained and go to school; they don't need her every second. She remembers thinking maybe she would call Helen if she could call Helen, but if she had been able to call Helen, she might have had the baby. If she knew that Helen would come to stay and sit up with Tess each night while she nursed, watch *Masterpiece Theatre* with her, bring her large, cold glasses of water, cook all her favorite meals. Tess doesn't want to be a new mother again without Helen there to help.

Josh shuffles the cards, and Martin scrolls through his phone, and Alice gets up to get a box of cookies from the pantry and takes three for herself and passes them around.

"What are we playing?" asks Henry.

"Canasta?" says Martin.

"Gin?" says Kate.

"We need a second deck for canasta," Tess says, hoping to dissuade them.

"Your lucky night," says Alice, reaching in the drawer under the table to find more cards.

"I'll deal," says Martin.

"What are the teams?"

"Couples?" Kate says.

"Sure," Tess says.

"You have to promise not to divorce me if we lose," Martin says to Tess.

"Or," says Tess, "we could just not lose."

Martin deals, Josh counts his cards three separate times, and Henry draws from the stock first, Alice after; they both discard and make their first meld of queens, and then it's Josh and Kate's turn and they each draw. Josh sets down three cards, a four, a five, and a six.

"They have to be the same," Martin says.

"They don't," Josh says.

"It has to be four cards," says Tess.

Josh gets out his phone, as do Alice and Martin. Tess gets up to grab the box of cookies and sits back in her chair and writes an email to a client.

"I was taught the European version," Josh says, holding up his phone screen.

"Of course," Tess mutters.

"We're playing the American one," says Henry.

"Maybe we shouldn't," Alice says.

"It's easier to play the rules we know," Martin says.

Josh reaches over Kate's shoulder and makes a meld of three kings and slaps them down and picks up his other cards, and they both discard.

"American it is," he says.

Kate and Josh win, and Alice watches Tess, but everybody seems to be having a good enough time, and Alice is glad that they're all here. She remembers how hopeful she was all those years ago when she and Henry got together. The way that he said the word "family": so different from that large, mostly silent house that she shared with her mom, and, less often, with her dad. Family was like religion to Henry, even when he didn't see them often. Even when they all annoyed him, when he complained about them each time after they left. Right up until she died, he talked to his mother on the phone more often than any grown-up Alice knew.

Alice grabs hold of her phone to check again for texts from Maddie, but instead there's an email from her mom confirming flights, a final plea to *have the privilege of seeing Henry too*.

She has what she figures is a much more normal relationship with her mother: she calls her once a month; they text. They send cards on birthdays, ask the same boring questions about their jobs. Mostly they resent each other from a comfortable enough distance that they might call it love.

At her wedding—which was not supposed to be a wedding, which was supposed to be a small party because they were moving to the city and they wanted all their friends to come together one more time in Maine before they left—Alice and her mother had fought. Sophie had gotten caterers and had a cake delivered;

Helen put the cake that she had baked away. Later, after Sophie flew back out west with Alice's father, when they were all out by the fire talking, Alice sitting next to Henry, his arm across her back, Helen had made fun of Sophie: *Does she know we don't think she's special because her husband's rich?* She wasn't wrong— but also, fuck Helen and that particular barb, *her husband*, when, had Sophie not pissed her off with the cake and some offhanded comment about Helen's homemade dress, had she not, in other words, felt like a threat, Helen would have been the first to say that calling the money only Alice's dad's was shitty and unfair. Had Alice not been so desperate for Helen to like her, she might have been less likely to hear Helen's derision as somehow also about her. She thought now that she'd thought then that she might shift, in all that time with Helen, that whatever alchemy her own mother had enacted on her in the years that she spent forming—*fix your face, please; not that shirt, please; could you please let your mother fix your hair; you cannot leave the house without at least some studs covering your ear holes;* the fingers tight around her upper arm, reminding her to smile—might be countered by the years she spent with Helen afterward. But then she had continued to feel separate, had not found a way of becoming any more or other than what she'd always been. It had not helped that she continued not to be a mother, when a mother was the thing that Helen had perhaps most fully been. It did not help that her reaction to the attempts that Kate or Helen made to call or visit, *to get to know her better,* often made her want to hide or disappear.

"We should teach the kids this game tomorrow," Kate says.

"They're too little," Tess says.

"When did you guys learn?" asks Josh.

"Young," Kate says. "It was the Christmas Henry ran away."

Henry sits up straighter. "'Ran away' seems strong."

"You ran away?" asks Alice.

"Not really." He sets his beer down, holds a hand up to his chin.

"You packed a bag," Kate says.

"What could you possibly have to run away from?" Tess pulls her sweater tight around her, puts her phone in the slat between the chair's cushion and the arm.

"I was asserting my autonomy."

"You were a spoiled brat," Kate says.

Martin takes one of the cookies. "Mom threw out his *collection*."

"I kept things under my bed."

"There were bird carcasses and dead lizards," Kate says. "It freaked her out. It smelled."

Henry takes a big swig of his beer and shakes his head at his little sister. "It was disgusting, but she still felt awful after," he says.

"Where did you run to?" asks Tess.

"I walked out to the beach to replace what she'd thrown out."

Kate wipes the ring on the table that Josh's beer's left. "You scared the shit out of Mom."

"I was fine; I didn't go that far."

Martin leans forward. "The beach was three miles from the house. I'd never seen her that angry."

"*I'd* seen her that angry," Kate says.

"She was so *glad and grateful* that you were okay."

"Henry got away with everything," Kate says.

"Still does," says Alice.

"We were kids. Not my fault you all never grasped the art of subtlety."

"You mean selfishness?" Kate says.

"I mean she let me off the hook more often because I didn't need as much from her."

"She was still paying your car insurance when you were thirty," Martin says.

"I mean emotionally. I didn't feel the need to call her every day."

"She liked that I called her every day," says Kate.

"I didn't make her responsible for my daily mental health."

Alice grabs his arm. "Enough, Henry."

"You scared the shit out of her on a near daily basis for most of your adult life," Kate says. "Out in the middle of nowhere doing fuck-all with your *brilliant brain*. With your history of depression."

"Who are we talking about now?"

"I showered," Kate says. "I had jobs."

"What exactly do you think jobs are proof of? Because I wasn't making money, I was worthless and lost?"

"She worried about you."

"She worried about us all."

Kate deals the cards, and Henry stares intently, craning his neck toward the backyard-facing window.

"Are you cheating?" Josh says.

"You're kidding, right?" says Henry.

"Never mind," Josh says, and gets up and leaves the table.

Alice passes Tess and Kate the last two cookies, and Josh comes back from the kitchen, where he's found another beer. Kate takes it from him once he sits down, takes a sip.

"Should we talk about the house now?" Tess says, phone in hand. "The realtor who did the rental for us said getting it on the market should go pretty seamlessly."

Alice undoes and folds the cookie box, and Martin moves from the floor to the one remaining chair. He takes the phone from Tess.

"We wanted to talk about that," Kate says. Josh takes his beer back, moves closer to her.

"We need to get some photos of the property," says Tess.

"We thought we might live in the house a while first," Kate says. "We thought . . . we wanted to ask you guys if . . ."

"You don't live in Florida," Tess says.

"We'd move there," Kate says. "The schools are really good in the area and . . ."

"How long's 'a while'?" Martin says.

Kate looks at Josh, who nods, his hand close to her knee.

"We thought," says Kate.

"We thought we'd bring the kids up there," Josh says. "It would mean a lot to Kate, you know, to raise our kids in the house where your mom raised you."

"The house is worth six hundred thousand dollars," Tess says. "I've seen the other sales close by. If that's what you guys want, you can buy us out." She looks straight at Josh.

"We don't need to break it down right now," Martin says.

"We don't have four hundred thousand dollars," says Josh.

"Since when?" Tess says.

"Since Josh's inheritance ran out." Kate angles her body away from Josh, will not mention the tech stocks. "We don't have that kind of money anymore."

"Well, you own the house in Richmond, don't you?"

Kate works to keep her face still. They refinanced to send the boys to a Montessori when Jack got suspended from the public school for the third time for biting. "We owe more than it's worth."

"We all have more expenses than we thought we would," says Tess.

"You make a pretty solid living, Tess," Kate says.

"We have a mortgage; Colin's therapist is three hundred and fifty dollars a week; Martin—"

Martin stops her: "It makes the most sense to just sell the house and go our separate ways."

"*Our separate ways?*" says Kate.

"We're not breaking up, Kate. It makes sense to split it evenly, especially if you all need money."

Tess leans farther forward in her chair and turns to Kate, her body close to Martin's. "It's what's fair, Kate. It's the cleanest, clearest, fairest thing."

"But what if we need it more than you do?" Kate says. "The house, the money, it means different things to different people. There are other ways to think of fair."

"I'm not sure it's fair to punish us for having jobs."

"I have a job, Tess," Josh says.

Tess sits up straighter, looking at Josh. "What would you do if you all moved to Florida? You wouldn't have a job if you moved."

"I have some leads."

"It means something to me, Tess, to raise my kids where we

lived," Kate says. "It means something to me to live in the house where our mom lived." Kate will not give Tess the satisfaction of crying. If she cries, Tess will say to Martin later how Kate always plays the victim-baby-little-sister, and Kate will not let Tess talk about her like that even if she doesn't have to be there when she does.

Josh grabs her leg, and in that moment she's grateful to him, forgives him for losing all that money. "We went down there," he starts.

"You've been down there in the past few months?" Tess interrupts. "To Helen's house? And you didn't tell any of us?"

It was perfect, Kate doesn't say. The brine-salt smell, the heat, the way her skin felt crisp, the flat glass of the water after a storm: it was the closest she'd been to something besides sad in months.

"We got an Airbnb," Josh says. "We synced it with the renters fall vacation; I went through with a contractor Kate knows."

"You should have said something," says Tess, turning to Kate.

"We wanted to get an idea of the work it might need," Josh says. "The roof is shot; the living room floor is slanted. We would fix it up. I could do most of that work myself."

She'd been proud, Kate, watching Josh move through the rooms, crawling underneath the house to check the ductwork, taking notes. It felt thrilling, a thing they'd do—a thing Josh would do—for all of them.

"You're not a structural engineer, Josh," Tess says.

"He's done most of the work on our house in Richmond," Kate says, emboldened. "He's learned sort of an insane amount from YouTube. We'd get it into shape, make twice as much in fifteen years."

"The place will most likely be underwater then," Henry says.

"That house is a teardown," Tess says. "No amount of DIY is going to make it otherwise." She pulls her sweater tighter, arms crossed and hands up by her shoulders. "We're asking people to pay for a plot of land ten minutes from the beach that, for now at least, is still worth a lot. In five years the storm and flood insurance could be prohibitive."

"Tess," says Martin.

"I was in touch with the state about it," Henry says.

"Jesus Christ," says Josh.

"It's relevant," says Henry, setting his beer down on the coffee table. "You're all so busy thinking about how to get the most bang for your investment."

"We're not giving the only asset we have to the state," Josh says.

Henry stands up, arms crossed. "The state has money. They could buy it. The house is backed up to a federal preserve. They could restore it as wetlands."

"It's an acre, Henry." Josh looks back at Kate. "The wetlands will not be saved because of it."

Henry's hand goes toward his face then out in front of him. "We could make an effort, though—a *contribution*."

Kate says: "What about the contributions we could make to send our kids to college?"

"You think you have more say because you have kids?"

"The stakes are different for us," Kate says. "As parents." From the corner of her eye she sees Tess look at Alice. Alice gets up and goes into the kitchen.

"You think your kids won't benefit from your giving a shit?" says Henry.

"We give a shit," says Martin.

"The state would pay, is all I'm saying," says Henry. "It might be below market, but there are things to consider beyond your fucking bottom line."

"Exactly," Kate says. "Like our family, our mother—like keeping the house in our family."

"Most of us," Tess says, "live in New York."

"But it could stay the place we go," Kate says. "It could stay the place we go when we all come together. I don't know how to ask you to understand that there is value to that for us."

Tess crosses her arms, leans forward, then back. "Don't do that, Kate. Don't be like that."

"Do what? I'm asking you to think about what mattered to our mother."

"I think what mattered to your mother was all of us."

"She loved that house, Tess."

"She loved us."

Henry has hold of Alice, who's come back with a beer and sits against him, her beer held tight with all ten fingers. "I think maybe this is enough grown-up bonding for our first night," Henry says.

"We have to settle this," says Josh.

"We will," says Martin. "But we also need to sleep. We don't need to wake the kids."

Kate doesn't look at any of them. She listens, eyes out the window, head angled toward the floor, as Tess and Martin go upstairs, as Alice and Henry get up together and walk out the back door.

• • •

"We don't get as much say because we don't have children," says Alice, lighting a cigarette and walking past the barn toward the woods. She doesn't really care what happens, but still, fuck them.

"No one said that," says her husband.

"Your fucking snail kites," she says.

When Henry was little, he has told her, from his upstairs window, looking out over the federal preserve, he'd watched them, only found in Florida in the U.S.: taloned raptors, beaks made to eat the snails found only in the wetlands; the only species of raptor that lived communally. He wants to make more space for all of them: the great blue herons, the ospreys, the bald eagles that he glimpsed sometimes when he was a kid.

"There aren't that many left," he says. She only started to smoke again last year, and she knows he hates to watch her do it, like she no longer cares what might or might not kill her. He looks back toward the barn instead. "I'm not sure why you think what I want matters less."

"Because they're trying to survive, Henry. My mom helped us. Your mom helped us. We have this house."

"Oh, fuck that," he says. "They're all rich. Their kids' futures aren't going to be determined by where they fucking go to college."

Alice smokes and waits for him to settle.

"When did my siblings become such gross people?"

"They're not gross, Henry. They're parents. They're trying to give their kids the lives they think they should have."

Later, Alice watches as Henry walks back to the barn. She goes back into the house by herself. He hugged her, held her. He can't help it, she thinks, leaving her like this.

...

Tess sends a few more work emails, and Martin manages not to tell her that she shouldn't look at screens in bed.

Josh follows Kate up the stairs and puts Bea back in bed next to her brothers. He reaches an arm around Kate's waist, and she waits for him to fall asleep so she can wriggle out from underneath and watch a baking show on her phone to settle down the whirring in her brain.

Henry wishes, thinking about his mother, about her house and those perfect gorgeous birds in her backyard—as he walks out to the barn, already grateful for the quiet and the dark, the long expanse of blank white snow he has to cross—Henry wishes he could sit outside with her under the stars. He wants to sit and explain to her, as he never did when she was alive, how beautiful it was, when he was little, body flat and still on the high, wet grass of their backyard, the squish of soil: a flock, a pack, a bunch of birds would swoop down and up, soar by, and he'd stay quiet. How they all moved together in one fluid bunch, as if they were a larger organism, not quite separate, as if they intuited one another's needs, their wants.

Everything he reads about this behavior focuses on efficiency, sensing and responding to the various magnetic pulls beneath the earth, but he's not interested in efficiency, has always hated the idea of it. It feels like more than that, and that's the part he wants to get right in his work—the part he wishes he could explain to his mother, to maybe ask her to help him understand it: the beauty of it, the inexplicable impossibility of their togetherness. How it cannot possibly be only about the wind and energy conservation. Eons before this, augurs used to divine omens in these flight patterns—he wishes he could tell his mother—it's a simple fact of nature but also otherworldly, as close as he will ever get to faith.

Once, after they had lost their father—Henry'd just met Alice, Martin and Tess had gotten married at city hall and had a small party at a restaurant, Josh and Kate were just out of college—they all went camping on the land where Henry lived with Alice in the yurt he'd built. Helen planned it. Helen talked to each child individually and over a period of weeks until she'd convinced them all to come, to take trains and rent cars and take off work. Henry and Alice lived up on a high ridge that overlooked a pond, and they all had their own tents. They brought big jugs of water and they built fires and they sat outside and talked and, against everybody's better judgment, they had fun.

The last night, Helen laid out blankets on the ground and forced them all to stay up late. They kept the fire going until close to midnight, and then she put it out and made them all stretch out on the ground. *Mom,* the boys said. They weren't boys, of course, but they sounded like it, when they said her name like that. *Just do it,* she said. *Jesus. Can't you just do as I say when I ask?* And Martin rolled his eyes, and Henry laughed and touched her up by the shoulder, and she smiled because she knew that they'd all finally give in. They lay down then, the lot of them, Tess annoyed and tired but also wanting all of them to like her, Josh saying something about ticks. But then a rush of stars had burst before them. You could make out the whole Milky Way from where they were. And minutes passed, and they all kept looking up, and a second shower of stars burst, shocking in their brightness and speed, appalling in how close they felt.

They'd all lain there, still and quiet, no one talking, no one arguing finally, grateful to Helen for making them all come together, for forcing them to lie on the ground in the middle of the night and look.

Henry has spent his whole life trying to make art, he wishes now that he could tell his mother, that felt like what it felt like lying there.

5

Colin's missing.

Tess is sweating, panting. She hadn't meant to run that long, but she couldn't sleep and went out before five. It was dark out. She forgets, when they're out of the city, that there are no lights that early in the morning. She used her phone's flashlight and hugged the shoulder of the road because there also weren't sidewalks. She wore the netted metal and it felt incredible. Instead of being scared the whole time that she might slip, instead of having always to be careful, her feet grabbed hold of the ice and sprang off.

The moon glinted off all the white and made it feel less dark. She ran eight miles, and only one car passed her. It was difficult to gauge the width of the road's shoulder, and also, she imagined the car couldn't see her, and she'd jumped down in a ditch as it drove by. As she got back, she felt much better, resolved to be better: to Kate, to Josh, to Martin; all five of the children. She resolved to do what she knew Helen would want. Kate is in pain, she convinced herself by mile six, she's sad and misses her mom and she's tired because Josh is useless, because whatever bit of security his money used to offer them is gone. By mile seven, she'd convinced herself that she should use all the energy she uses hating Josh being more generous to Kate and all the kids instead, that she should consider, at least, what they want.

But now her son is gone, and there is nothing else but that.

When she left an hour ago, both kids were still passed out on the air mattress. She'd taken a picture of them with her cell phone: the two of them so peaceful, bodies close to one another, still.

Now, it's only Stella. Tess has searched the whole upstairs. She runs downstairs but quiet, barefoot, as if, if she doesn't wake up anybody else, Colin won't actually be gone. She checks the bathroom. She will not get frantic. She'll find him, she feels sure, and she doesn't want to later hear from Martin about how overly anxious she always gets. Inexplicably, she checks the kitchen cabinets. She whisper-calls her son's name throughout the ground floor of the house.

She walks down to the basement. It's unfinished. She checks the bathrooms, puts her shoes back on, a coat over her sweaty shirt and tights, and heads outside.

"Colin," she yells, not caring any longer if she wakes the others. "Baby," she says, quiet. She wants to break into a run again but reminds herself that that won't help, that she wouldn't know which way to go. The woods loom behind the house, acres of them, looking cold and dark. The highway sits on the other side. The snow is deeper back here, and her shoes are soaked, as are her tights up to her thighs.

"Colin," she says, louder now, but all she sees are trees and snow, and she bounds toward the street calling his name.

• • •

Kate hears Tess outside calling to Colin and leaves the room without waking the children. She looks at them, their perfect still and sleeping bodies, all three of them so close to one another. She takes a picture with her phone to look at later when they're up and yelling, pulls her boots on in the mudroom and her coat on over her flannel pajamas. They're festive, red and green, and as soon as she's outside the house she pulls her coat tight around so Tess won't see.

She runs to Tess. "Where is he?" she says.

"I don't know," Tess says, frantic, sweaty. "He isn't in the house."

They stare too long at one another. Kate hates feeling helpless; she knows that Tess hates needing. They both call Colin's name at the same time, and Kate sees a light on in the barn and walks over. The doors are large and heavy, and it takes a while to get one open. She has to pull a piece of wood out of another piece of wood, and then it rolls down on a hinge and she has to pull the door instead of push and then there's light and cold and the kiln's acrid, tangy smell and a high and wide expanse of space and her big brother, up close to the ceiling, flat on his back, his arms up in the air, Colin still and quiet on the scaffolding at his side.

Tess hears Kate calling from the barn.

I found him.

She won't let herself be sure until she has Colin. She bounds through the big, open door, and then he's there, her boy, still in his pajamas with his coat on over top of them, up high next to Henry, boots on, smiling at her, fiddling with thick pulley-rigged strings. Her boy, she thinks, and breathes.

She whispers thanks to Kate, but she's not sure she hears.

. . .

Kate waits a while, watching Tess fret over Colin. There's a sheet covering most of Henry's work, but she likes the look of him, stronger and more confident, up there in the air. If Martin is the brother that cared for Kate, kept her safe, checked on her in college once a week after their dad died to make sure she wasn't getting into trouble, Henry is the brother that Kate's always loved the most. He was quiet but always watching—unfazed mostly, stoic until he got older. Once, growing up, teenaged, driving past a gated community close to their Florida house, he told her he wanted to napalm the place. *Entitled fucking rich people,* he said, *destroying our planet because they'll always be safe.* She didn't know what he was saying. She knew what napalm was, and she also knew that her family wasn't rich but neither were they poor and that her brother was self-righteous even then. While Martin went and got a job and then a spouse like other people, while Kate did the same, Henry lived alone in the woods of Maine and only talked to Helen, only ever really cared about his work that wasn't work in any grown-up sense. He'd met Alice up there, right after she finished art school. Henry never went to art school. Useless, he said, worthless networking, a waste of time.

Alice was beautiful and smart; Kate could hardly look at her when they met. When she did, she couldn't help but stare, so she tried to not be in the same room with her for too long. It wasn't only her appearance but her power over Henry. She got him to leave the woods when no one else, not even Helen, could. She got him to move to New York, which he'd spent his whole life saying was where people went to pretend to be whatever they'd set out to be instead of being it. He would still say that for most of the time he lived there, but he liked Alice more than he hated New York. And in the city, he had friends, endless rounds of friends who got him "gigs" when he needed money. He helped build sets for film shoots, read out loud to a blind man, moved art from warehouses to museums, did permitless construction jobs.

Kate was thrilled by the stories he told her, by his and Alice's always too-cold, art-filled tiny studio close to the water, the stunning, arid art of their friends on their walls. Before she and Josh were married, she'd stay with Henry and Alice occasionally even though Martin and Tess's place had a whole extra bedroom. She'd sleep on the couch beneath their lofted bed, and they'd go out late and walk home together, drunk, over the Williamsburg Bridge.

When Alice told her, just after the twins were born, that they were "trying," Kate hadn't known what she meant at first. To make more art, to be more successful, she thought. This was not long after Alice's Big Show that Kate had come to, early in her third trimester. It had been stunning, she thought: massive, dark collages. That evening, she had kept sneaking looks at Alice, her tall, thin frame, across the room, attempting to imagine how she'd made such huge, beautiful things on her own. There was a precision to it up close, *meticulous,* Kate kept thinking, which was a word she didn't say out loud to anyone in case it was wrong.

Kate's life then was loose and messy, murky, the specific drudgery of having a small child and two on the way—she'd quit already to get ready—shapeless days that all felt the same. In the months that followed, she'd mostly disappeared inside the endless morass that was her kids' wants and needs. She didn't mind this, though, mostly; she quite liked it, though this was not something that she often shared. It was a relief, in fact, knowing so clearly every day what her tasks were, that they were worthwhile, dull and mushy but also intimate and private, solid; Kate could tell no one other than Helen how much she liked being a mother. It was not the motherhood that wore Kate out, it was the shame she felt for wanting only to be that.

Alice brews the coffee and grills an egg and bread. Whatever's happening outside, there are plenty of grown-ups. She doesn't want to talk to Henry, wants nothing more than to talk to Henry.

When they first met, she couldn't get enough of him. He was everything everyone she met in art school wasn't: determined, single-minded, completely uninterested in talking about himself. He worked all day and night, and this was also new to Alice. She had been shocked, the whole time she was in grad school, by how little actual work her colleagues did. They did so much more *talking* about work, drinking; they slept with one another. None of this interested Alice. She worked and sometimes, when it interested her, she engaged. Other times, she stayed quiet in the back. She wanted to make something no one else had, something Big, Important, though she would not ever have admitted this to anyone. She thought for a long time that she might make work that lasted. But the truth was, no one needed art the way they needed food and shelter. No one needed art the way they needed to be kept alive.

It still shocks her sometimes to see how fully Henry forges on. It feels embarrassing. She remembers it, though: getting up early and still bleary, the need, the feeling that it was the only place where she had control, the idea that she could make material, real, and whole what had before felt and been only abstract. Just before she stopped, she was working with dark oils on big canvases. She did dark, broad strokes and then spent hours reshaping, shading and upending, making smaller, sharper lines she'd linger over for weeks or months. She'd felt close to something, manic in the way work made her manic, circling a small, calm, quiet space amidst the chaos and then order and then chaos and then order of the work. She had a show in a big gallery, a good gallery, a gallery in Chelsea about which all her friends were proud and probably also jealous. She got a review in the *New York Times* that called her work "important," "riveting." If she had told twenty-three-year-old her that any of this would happen, she would have felt ecstatic, breathless; what else was there to want but that? Not much of the work sold, though, and the review was, predictably, about Alice's Blackness, though she was half Black, though she'd grown up mostly raised by her white mother. Though her mother's only engagement with her Blackness had been to help her learn to straighten and relax her hair, to compliment, each time she saw her, the beauty and the smoothness of her skin. Of course, Alice knocked up every day in different ways with her not-whiteness, with all the ways that she felt separate, looked at but not seen or understood, without the language or the resources, without the people, to help her make sense of this large part of who she was. The reviewer seemed transfixed by the *pain* he saw in the work, the *rawness* of it. Alice had never thought much about her work in relation to that word; she'd been thinking mostly about technique and form.

"Fuck rawness," Alice said to Henry when he read the review

to her over coffee at the place close to their apartment. "'Raw' is code for their thinking I didn't do the work. For solipsism that they'll let slide because I'm Black."

From the critics, there was no talk of the work she'd put in to craft the pieces precisely, to put the parts together. She'd torn strips out of the canvases and repurposed them on different canvases. She'd painted in a fury, messy, anxious strokes, and then broken them up in jagged rips and put them back together in precise, specific forms. But there was no talk of that. The focus instead was on the angry mess, the fury and the feeling. Alice's parents were wealthy, educated; her dad was a banker; she had gone to private schools, then Yale. The reviewer could have googled this, and yet he seemed intent on seeing something elementally persecuted, oppressed in her work. Which, maybe, she thought later—bringing the unsold work back to their apartment from the gallery—probably, there was.

It was shitty, the questions people asked in grad school about the origins of her work, her intentions, how her "background" informed what she did. Her parents had told her from a young age not to pay attention to these questions and these conversations. She was brilliant, pretty, special, *privileged,* regardless of her skin color. She wished now that they hadn't lied so much.

Quinn's up early, cleaning the kitchen and looking out the back window, rinsing the two bowls streaked with grease and Parmesan from the night before. She has to get the presents wrapped. She waits for the coffee grounds to steep in the French press; presses. Years ago, at one of the restaurants where she worked, she was converted to the French press; likes the feel of it even more than she notices the difference in the coffee's taste: the pouring of the water, the slow, deliberate way the grounds slide down the edges of the glass. Maddie's door is closed, and she doesn't check on her for fear of waking her before she gets the wrapping done and the presents rehidden on the shelf in her closet above her sweaters. The shelf is just above the drawer inside a drawer where the three pills still are.

The place feels cold this early in the morning; Quinn's sad all of a sudden that she let Maddie talk her out of a Christmas tree. Maddie refused a tree because of *the climate*. Quinn isn't sure this makes sense, but also, she doesn't question Maddie when it comes to facts about the world. She's obsessed, maybe, Maddie, with *the climate*. She asks about sea levels rising at least once a week; she asks about hurricanes, fires, and floods. Quinn is often scared by what her daughter says, and by her own lack of answers. Quinn used to google Maddie's questions about climate just as she did all the other questions Maddie asked for which she had no answers. But when she googled *the climate,* everything either horrified her or made no sense. Now she just nods when Maddie talks about it and agrees with her. When Maddie asks questions, Quinn tells her to look it up and hands her her phone. She thinks now she should have overridden her, put some block on the phone's Wi-Fi. She should have gotten a fake tree. But Maddie said the footprint of all that fake shit, all that waste, wasn't worth the ritual (though Maddie didn't say "fake shit"). It's the ritual, though, that Quinn wishes she could give her now.

There are presents, at least. They've not played at the pretense of Santa since Maddie was four. They'll watch the same movie that they always watch on Christmas, Holly Hunter, Robert Downey Jr., *Home for the Holidays,* a movie that was made the year that Quinn was born. It's too grown-up for Maddie, maybe, but then Maddie's always felt more grown up to Quinn than Quinn herself.

She gets a stool and gets the presents down, gets the wrapping paper, scissors, tape. She sits cross-legged on her bed, quiet. Maddie's fourth Christmas was the Christmas that they spent apart: her social worker—*Alice, call me Alice, please, Quinn,* her perfect, pretty face too close to hers, always acting like they should pretend that they were friends—came the week before and picked up Maddie's gifts. She had supplemented them, Quinn found out later, when Maddie wrote Quinn a card to thank her for the gifts and mentioned books, a pair of shoes Quinn hadn't bought. This year, she wraps a model rocket ship and a pair of shoes with planets on them that were too expensive and which Maddie will grow out of by March. She has a book on birds, a book on space, a book about four sisters recommended for her online called *The Penderwicks*. She is terrible at wrapping, and the corners are all crooked and she keeps one eye angled toward the door so Maddie doesn't catch her, keeps quiet so she can hear when Maddie starts to stir.

Tess leaves Colin in the barn with Henry, *working with him,* he says. She goes back in to check on Stella, who's with Martin, eating pancakes, telling him a story about a *Troodon*.

"Everything okay?" says Martin.

She doesn't want to tell on Colin. "All good," she says. She's not angry at him any longer; her run calmed her, loosened her a little. Maybe later she'll ask Martin if they should talk to Kate about some sort of compromise for Helen's house.

"You hungry?" he says.

Tess goes to grab hold of Stella, but her daughter pulls away before Tess can get her arms around her. "You're sweaty," Stella says. "You stink."

"Colin's outside?" says Martin.

Tess keeps her eyes on Stella. "*Working* with his uncle Henry in the barn."

Martin takes Stella's fork and eats a large piece of pancake, nodding toward her. "Of course," he says. "Important work."

Tess kisses Stella's forehead, smiles at Martin. She goes upstairs to the large bathroom and peels off her clothes, pulls her hair out of its rubber band. There's a space heater in the corner, and she turns it on. She stretches, naked, as she waits for the water to warm up, raises her arms high up over her head and bends in each direction, rolls her shoulders back. Steam comes from the shower, and she goes in and stands a long time underneath it. Most of the good work from the run was undone by the thing with Colin. Even though he was completely fine, helping Henry with the pulley system, thatching thin pieces of wood to connect the birds, though Henry had strung a large spread of sheets across the ceiling so they couldn't see the end result. Colin claimed to have seen the light out in the barn and gone out to find his uncle. The house has a large backyard but is right up against a major road, and when she left him out there to come inside, she made him promise to go straight from the barn to the house when he came in. He'd nodded as she spoke but refused to look directly at her, and she feels unsure now—sometimes when she talks to him she truly does not know whether he took in anything she said.

• • •

Kate flips pancakes for her children. Martin mixed the batter, tripled the Fannie Farmer cookbook recipe that all Helen's children know by heart, but he only cooked enough for his kids, left the bowl with the remaining batter by the stove. Bea ate Colin's plate, and now the boys have just come downstairs and are wailing that they're hungry and why has no one fed them.

Kate watches Josh out the window with his igloo again, the light behind him from the barn. In the barn, with Henry, the little that she'd glimpsed beneath the sheets had been both beautiful and strange, what looked like tiny clay painted birds stretching across the ceiling. Even as Tess rushed in, as she grabbed hold of Colin, pulled him off the scaffolding to hug him, as Kate watched him flinch and Tess stepped back, embarrassed, was clearly close to tears, Kate worked to catch glimpses of them: the birds looked more real than they should have, the textures of their feathers alive and delicate somehow.

"Big plans for today?"

Kate jumps and turns to see her middle brother. "I thought you'd work all day."

Henry nods toward Alice, who stands separate from them, on her second cup of coffee. "I am under strict instructions to be bonding during waking hours."

"Lucky us," Kate says. She sidles closer to the stove so Henry can wash the paint from his hands in the sink. They both watch the pancakes bubble on the griddle.

"You really want to go to Florida?" he says.

"It's where we're from," says Kate. "Mom loved it there."

"We hated it," he says. He turns and gets a stack of plates for her.

She flips the pancakes, piles up two stacks on the plates that Henry's holding. "*You* hated it."

He brings the food to her boys and kisses the top of each of their heads.

"Thank you, Uncle Henry," Kate says.

"Thank you, Uncle Henry," both boys say.

"It's so . . . Republican," he says.

"It's conservative," she argues, pouring both boys a glass of water. "But Mom's friends aren't. She wasn't."

"You're going to hang out with Mom's friends?"

"We'd find other friends," she says.

He takes the pan from her and wipes it clean, starts in on the mixing bowl and Bea's and Stella's plates.

"Besides, since when do you have friends?" she adds.

They both watch as the boys dig into their pancakes, as Jack dips two fingers into the pool of syrup and licks and dips again.

"You want to raise them there, though?" Henry says.

"Our childhood was good."

"But we left."

"When I was twenty-two I needed to prove I could leave, but who actually cares? I made things harder on purpose, leaving—without Mom, learning the Richmond weather and Richmond schools, that place and those people's expectations—it feels insane. So dumb."

"I'm out of syrup," Jamie says.

"How do you ask?" Kate says, though Henry's already pouring. "I wish we'd gone back years ago," she says.

Outside, the light is perfect. They've passed to the other side of early morning, and in the flat expanse of yard between the back of the house and the barn the sun's light skates and slides across the snow.

"You're sure this isn't some crisis?" says Henry. "A grief response or something. What if a year from now you wake up horrified you turned your whole life upside down?"

"What life, though, Henry?" Kate says. She turns from the window toward him. "I take the kids to school. I do the laundry. I make the breakfasts and the lunches and the dinners. I can do that anywhere. I want to do it where I can give my kids as good as what we had."

"But what about . . ." She sees him straining, her big brother, wanting to make more of her life, to elevate it, like he always wants to elevate things, into something more special and ambitious than it actually is. She looks out the window again, past the barn into the woods, *stick season,* Alice calls it. Most of the leaves are missing, the stolid trunks and the reaching, overlapping branches jut. She should bundle the kids up and take them out to show them, bring her phone and take a picture of how clean and perfect it all looks.

"It's not bad, you know," she says to Henry. "It's not all awful drudgery—my kids, my husband. I have people I can talk to; I can find other people I can talk to. Josh still makes me laugh."

The boys have finished eating, and she calls to them to wash their hands as they ignore her and escape upstairs to find their cousins. Kate picks up both plates, and Henry takes them, cleans them.

"The beach is nice," he says. "Bea would be killer on a surfboard."

"Think how much fun we had," she says. "And I need it, Henry. A shift. A change. I need to feel close to her in some way. I need that house more than the birds do."

. . .

Alice checks her phone for texts from Maddie, lights a cigarette again outside. Yesterday she baked a bunch of slabs of gingerbread for a gingerbread house project—Helen used to do this—but she doesn't feel up to the mess of it quite yet. She wants to sit all day out here and not talk to any of them. It's Henry's family, she thinks. Henry can take care of it.

"Pointless, probably," Josh says. "To say you shouldn't do that." He nods toward her cigarette.

He's come up behind her suddenly, and she stops herself from flinching, pulls hard on her cigarette. "Definitely not worth your time," she says.

He pulls both gloves off and inspects them, then stuffs them in his coat pockets and runs his hands together, blowing on them. "Got a fucking hole in my gloves," he says.

"Henry might have an extra pair somewhere," she says.

"Are they Gore-Tex?"

"No idea."

"Those three can't help but act like kids when they're together," he says.

"You mean your wife?" she says.

"All three of them," he says. "My wife, your husband. Martin. We could make that house worth twice as much."

"Josh," she says, "I don't want to talk about this now." She finishes her cigarette and stubs it out on the side of the house, looking past Josh toward the woods.

"You know, that igloo," he says, nodding toward it, "it can get up to sixty-seven degrees inside it. I watched this YouTube thing about it last week."

"Very cool," she says, wishing he'd just leave her.

"It is," he says. "I think it is."

...

"You guys!" Tess calls to the kids as Alice gets out gingerbread slabs to make houses. It's too early for this much sugar, but Tess wants to keep the children close.

Kate pours the candy into bowls, and Alice gets blunt knives to spread the frosting. Tess gets each kid settled with six slabs of gingerbread and enough frosting to connect each of the parts. "Colin, stop it," she says, as he pops a third piece of candy into his mouth.

"Jack already ate a whole bowl."

"You're the oldest."

"So I'm punished for being old?"

"I empathize," says Martin, coming up behind him, taking a piece of candy.

"You won't have anything to decorate your house with," Tess says, ignoring Martin.

"I don't care about the stupid house."

Bea cries because her house keeps caving in, and the boys give up and each eat one of their walls. They throw gummy cherries at one another, laughing. Jamie has red frosting in his hair, and Jack licks it off. Kate holds Bea's hand and uses her other hand to hold the walls in place. "It's going to be beautiful," she says.

"It's not," Bea says. "It's ruined."

Kate squeezes the walls harder. She feels like she might cry too. It's all, it's always, so much less than she thought it would be when they started. The gumdrops are all crooked, the colors are too dull. The candy cane they placed in the middle of the roof fell through and is stuck now, cracked down the middle, so that the roof is much higher on the left. Alice put food coloring in two of the bowls of frosting, and Bea spread it on the wall's sides, but the heat is on too high and the frosting's melted, drooping. There's too much candy on one wall.

"It's going to be perfect," Kate says, looking at Bea, still holding her hand. She lets go of the wall and leans back. The walls droop more, list, but they don't fall, and Kate reaches into the back pocket of her jeans to get her phone. "See?" she says, nudging Bea into the frame and trying to find an angle that makes the house look less sad. "A masterpiece."

"Men Very Easily Make Jugs Serve Useful Needs, Perhaps," says Maddie. "That includes Pluto. As does: My Very Eager Mother Just Served Us Nine Pizzas; My Very Educated Mother Just Sat Upon Nine Porcupines; My Very Energetic Mother Jumps Skateboards Under Nana's Patio; Many Volcanoes Emit Mulberry Jam Sandwiches Under Normal Pressure."

She still wears her pajamas, socked feet, on the couch close to Quinn. Quinn was able to get all the presents wrapped.

"My Violent Evil Monster Just Scared Us Nuts is without Pluto, since she was declared a dwarf planet. That's sort of a scary one."

Quinn's charmed by Maddie's assuming Pluto's a she, finds it extra sad, the way she got pushed out.

"My Very Elegant Mother Just Served Us Nachos," Maddie says.

"I like that one," says Quinn.

"My Very Easy Memory Jingle Seems Useless Now. Many Very Educated Men Justify Stealing Unique Ninth."

"What is stealing ninth?"

"That one's not very good."

"Aside from Pluto, which is your favorite?"

"I hate favorites."

"Tell me why you like each one."

Maddie gets one of her planet books, and Quinn scrolls through her phone. Her ex-boyfriend has posted pictures of some girl she knows he knows from work. She opens Chrome and signs in to her mom's Facebook and there are a whole bunch of new notifications since last night; there's a whole new album of pictures posted on her wall. Quinn has to be careful not to mark anything that hasn't been read as read, to disable the chat while she scrolls through. She sees photos of a small house set close to the street. Two empty bedrooms, a bathroom with an old clawfoot tub. Apparently Quinn's mom moved out of the house she and Quinn lived in together. Quinn feels sure a man's involved; her mother does not have the money to buy a house. Maybe getting rid of Quinn really did make her life better. Maybe now that she's free she's found all the things that she could never get when she had Quinn. *Not everything is about you,* is what her mom would say when she was little, what her mom would no doubt say to her now. But it feels like it's about her, the fact that this house is so much nicer than the one they lived in together, an upgrade after all those years of hating that small, airless house where she grew up.

You're the one who ran away, Quinn tells herself. She tells herself this over and over, to make herself less angry. It feels jarring, though, still, the way her mother's life just keeps on going; the way she isn't frozen, shocked and devastated, by Quinn's not being there.

"Want to walk down to the foundry?" Quinn says, throwing her phone on the couch. "Fresh air?"

"I want to read," says Maddie.

"We have to move our bodies," Quinn says.

"I don't want to move my body."

"Animals?" Quinn says.

"I'm a bear," Maddie says. "Hibernating." But she lets Quinn pull her off the couch.

"We can split one of those pints of ice cream when we get home," Quinn says. "If you just go look for birds with me for an hour?"

6

The houses were a failure, Alice sees now, cleaning up the frosting and the candy. The frosting wasn't a strong enough adhesive. Stella's caved as soon as she got up to wash her hands, and Bea cried because hers barely held together in the first place. Colin and the twins left their walls all in a pile after eating half.

"Anybody want to go sledding?" Alice says, to make things better. There's a hill closer to town where kids go on snowy weekends. Alice is desperate to not have to talk to anyone for a while. If they go sledding she can stand quietly while the kids throw themselves down the hill.

"We need more than one car," Tess says.

"Henry and I can take them." Alice grabs hold of Henry. "Right?" she says, nodding at him. "They'll all fit in our car. Give you all a break."

"I could use the time to make one more call to Santa," Kate says, winking at Jack and Jamie, sweeping the last pile of their crumbled walls into a garbage bag.

"We could get started on the pie dough," says Martin, pouring what's left of the candy back into its container.

"I have some work I could catch up on," says Tess.

"Brilliant all around," Alice says. She grabs hold of Stella and Bea, nods toward Colin. "You guys go get ready, and I'll pack the car."

Kate leans her head against the cold car window. They're halfway to the outlets two towns over. Josh ripped a hole in his gloves making his igloo and needs a new pair. Kate got worried she has too many gifts for Bea and not enough for the twins.

Josh makes his Tess face—he squints his eyes and puckers his lips and looks stern and scoldy—and Kate laughs. She tightens her jaw, sucks her cheeks in, makes her Tess face back.

"Fair is fair," Josh says, shrilly.

Kate stops laughing. "She's not wrong, though," she says. "It's not fair, what we're asking for."

"Oh, fuck fair," says Josh. "They're all spoiled brats."

"It's not just money, though," she says. "They should . . . that house means more than that."

Out here it's ugly, highway, strip malls, all that brown and gray again. Kate wishes for the thousandth time that they were in Florida.

"I think Henry might be up for it," she says.

"We just have to prove to Tess that she'll still get her money in the end," he says.

"Fuck Tess," she says, which feels satisfying.

Josh laughs. "I do still have to find a job."

"I thought you said you had leads?"

"I know some people. That doesn't mean they want to give me a job."

"I could maybe . . ." Kate used to do design, the interiors of houses but also stores and restaurants. She was good at it. Her boss had called her four different times over the first year of the twins' lives—the last two she'd let go to voice mail—to make sure she hadn't changed her mind about coming back. She has a sudden image of putting on grown-up clothes, foundation and mascara, shoes that click as she heads out of the house; she thinks of whole hours in which her limbs aren't being grabbed at, clothes not being pulled on, sitting in an office, quiet.

"Who would take care of the children?" Josh says. "Make the lunches and the dinners, if you went back to work?"

"Is that a joke, Josh?" What she doesn't say is: *The only thing you ever had to do was keep the fucking money in the bank, and you could not.*

"You know what I mean . . . I'm no good at that stuff," he says. "We still have to eat."

"You could learn," she says, trying to stay light, to stay easy. "I have faith."

"So I'd be your kept man then? My father held my balls all these years, and now you'll take over till I'm dead?"

Kate thinks about the boys and Bea waiting after school for her to get them, all the plans she had for when they went to Florida, all the places that she'd take them after school. Josh's dad was an asshole, his mom quiet and submissive, not much help to her two children when his dad got mean and mad. He's wounded, she thinks now, her husband. It's her job to help him through. "We're partners, Josh," she says.

He pulls into the parking lot. It's crowded, and he has to drive down eleven different aisles of cars before he finds a spot. She zips her coat, and he zips his, and they both get out and close their doors. Josh presses the button, and the car beeps, and she stands close to him, and he grabs hold of her and brings his face close to hers. She knows that he feels pissed—inside him anger's churning, slowly unfurling—but to her, the way his face looks clenched and anxious, desperate, he looks sad.

He says: "I can find a fucking job."

"They went shopping?" Tess says to Martin. She's on the couch with her laptop, wrapped up in her favorite cardigan, her hair pulled up. She's relieved by the feel of the computer, fingers fast and firm on the keyboard, the force and clarity with which she is able to draft eleven emails, check in with a colleague, edit and prepare to file three motions, sign off on four more.

"They went to the outlets. Josh seemed to think there'd be good sales."

"You know that shit they make for the outlets is lower quality."

"Who cares?"

"I'm just talking, Martin. It doesn't matter," she says. What she doesn't say is: *I have to care because you've let me do all the worrying and the bitching—most of the money-making—for all of us.* "I'll just finish off some work here, you can roll Kate's pie dough, we can both enjoy the quiet."

"That doesn't sound so terrible," he says. He sits down next to her, and she tries to enjoy being close to him, the look and smell and feel of him, to remember that she likes being married to him. She tries to remember the last time they had sex, thinks maybe she should touch him, put down her computer, put her hand on his shoulder, flip her legs over his, hold his face, reach her hand down his pants.

"You don't seriously think we should just give them the house?" she says instead.

Martin moves closer to the window, farther from her. "I don't know, Tess. Can we not talk about it now?"

"We have to talk about it, Martin. It's two hundred thousand dollars."

"It's not just money."

"Perfect," she says. "So I'm the only cold, unfeeling one."

"That's not what I said."

"Your sister's playing you. Remember those stories you used to tell me? About when you were kids? Your mom would leave you alone, and you'd all scrap, hit one another, play-fight, and she'd be fine—and then three hours later, your mom would come home, and she'd lie on the floor and wail that you had hurt her. That's what she's doing now, except in grown-up form."

"She was six."

"People don't change that much."

"Maybe there's a middle ground. She's my sister, Tess. I don't want to fight with her."

"Of course not," she says. And then, knowing she's not being fair but saying it regardless, knowing that what makes her good at what she does—litigation—is her willingness, often, to push past what's fair or even precisely true, she says: "Anything but fight for us instead."

They stay too late, and it starts to get dark, and Alice feels sure Tess will be annoyed with her. She gets three texts from her: checking in. Each time, she sends a new photo of the kids to the family group text. Alice has snow in her boots, and her hands are wet from rolling snowballs, but it feels good, exhilarating, to move her body this way, to run, to be outside, to sweat. She watches Henry ride down the hill on the sled with Stella on his lap. Jamie and Jack chase after them on foot, Colin behind them on his own sled, screaming at them to slow down, his hat flying off his head. Bea comes up behind her with a snowball and throws it at her and Alice bends down, rolls a snowball of her own and throws back, but Bea ducks, runs toward her brothers, throws more snowballs at them.

Alice sees the two bodies from far away and tells herself it's not them, not to get her hopes up. But it is them, walking through town, close to one another, talking, laughing, happy: Maddie and Quinn.

"Who's that?" asks Stella, close behind her.

"Who?" asks Alice, starting.

"That," says Stella, pointing toward Quinn and Maddie.

"You shouldn't point at people," Alice says, pulling Stella's arm down.

"Who is it?" Stella says. She looks at Alice, rubbing her arm where Alice grabbed her. "That hurt."

"No one," says Alice, and immediately feels bad. "Sorry," she says, reaching for her. "It's just some people I know from work."

"I'm starved," says Colin, close behind them, his hat back on, cheeks flushed, the hair around his face wet with sweat and snow and stuck to his head. "I might die if you don't feed me now."

"Do you have snacks?" Jack asks, close behind his cousin, panting, pulling his brother behind him on the sled.

Alice rifles through her bag but she gave them all away at work last week.

"She's not a mom," says Bea, pulling two sleds and shaking

snow from her hair as she gets closer to them. "Non-moms never have snacks."

Tess stares out the window for the thousandth time. She watched from behind her computer as Martin followed Kate's instructions for the pie dough. Tess will never learn to cook, she understands now. *This could be your dish, Tess,* Helen would say at least once each time they saw her, Helen making lentils, arroz con pollo, some complicated casserole that she promised Tess *only had like six or seven steps.* She admired Tess, she said, how hard she worked; *always working,* she would mutter when Tess got out her computer after the kids were sleeping, not in a particularly admiring way. There was something fundamentally off-putting to Helen, Tess thought, about the fact that Martin did more of the domestic labor than Tess did. But Martin liked to cook, had learned from Helen. Despite Helen's disapproval, Martin's contributions to their household were also further proof of what a great mom Helen had been.

She's written ten more emails, and Martin's wrapped three clumps of pie dough in Saran Wrap, put them in the freezer, ordered them four pizzas. Still the kids aren't home. "Why is it so dark?" she says to Martin.

"Because it's winter," he says.

"I hate how dark it gets up here."

"Tess, they're fine. They're on their way. Enjoy the quiet." He comes up behind her, wraps his arms around her.

"Didn't she say they were just going into town?" she says.

"They're having fun, Tess. *Playing.*"

Lights fly by fast, but none of them turn in the driveway. Tess picks up her phone, looking for a text from Alice, but would also settle for an email to respond to. "It's been hours," she says.

Martin takes her phone out of her hand and puts his hands on her shoulders. "Does it make me a bad uncle," he says, "that I can't tell the twins apart?"

Tess laughs at him, slips out of his grasp. "Jamie is the calm one and he's shorter; he's shaped more like your sister."

"And Jack's tall and nuts like Colin."

"Please don't say that."

"Jack has *impulse control issues* like our son."

"He's sweet, too, you know? Our son. Desperate to please you."

"So you say," he says.

She shakes her head, frustrated. "None of us is perfect, Martin. For example, are we ever going to talk about your job?"

He turns to face her. "Admirable pivot, counsel," he says. "You said yourself that I did nothing wrong."

"Illegal. You didn't do anything illegal. You fucked up, though. You crossed a line." It all feels intimate and messy, even though he didn't sleep with anyone. It's the clarity with which she sees how little, actually, she knows about her husband's life, the sharpness and the shock of it. What it felt like, the day he told her, abashed and sorry and so separate, Tess rifling through the hours and hours when he could have been or done anything without her there to see him. That sickly, slippery feeling that she would never be safe really, that there was no one in the world that she could wholly trust.

"What do you want me to do about it? I told you I was sorry. I was stupid. What else is there to do or say?"

"I don't know, Martin."

"What do you want, Tess? Just tell me what you want me to do, and I will."

Kate finishes wrapping the last present, her corners perfect. They've just come back to find Tess and Martin looking chastened, were able to get upstairs without having to chat. Josh comes out of the shower and pulls on jeans and a shirt.

"The kids are almost here, I think," she says, seeing Alice's group text. Josh stands close to her. He's not said he's sorry but he pulled two weed gummies out of the glove compartment and stopped twice on the side of the road so she could take pictures of the mountains with her phone and post them on Instagram. It's his way of apologizing. "Can you help me put all this away?" She feels lighter now, a little giddy, from the weed.

They pile the presents on the highest closet shelf.

"What if they don't give it to us?" she says.

"We'll get a rental," he says. "If you really want to go to Florida we can find something. I'll find some sort of job eventually."

"We can't afford it," she says. "There is no rental market."

"We're renting your mom's house out right now. And we'll have extra money once we sell it."

"Everybody does Airbnb. How do you think Tess got so much for it?"

"So we'll get an Airbnb."

"That one we got when we went down was fifteen hundred a week." Her buzz from the gummy begins to dissipate.

"I don't know, Kate. Maybe we give up, then. Stay put."

Downstairs they hear the kids. Boots and coats and yells and screams and doors opening and closing. "Bathroom, Colin," they hear Tess say.

"Pizza, everybody," Martin calls from somewhere farther underneath them.

"Pizza," Josh says, smiling at her. He pulls another couple gummies from his pocket.

Kate tries to smile but she can tell it's crooked, sharp. She chews the gummy, looking at him. His hair's too long, she thinks. "I am going to make this happen, Josh."

"Maddie?" Quinn has to get the chicken fingers out of the toaster oven and shower and get the corn cooked. They only lasted an hour at the foundry; it was too cold. They didn't see a single bird. At home, Maddie sat on the couch and read and Quinn scrolled dejectedly again through her mother's Facebook page. Under every single picture of the new house was the same comment from stupid Sue from church: *Huge Congrats!!*

"Maddie," she says, louder. She walks down the hall into her daughter's room and finds her reading under the covers in a bundle on her bed. "*Maddie?*"

"Yeah?" Maddie still doesn't look up. As Quinn watches she turns a page.

"What the fuck?" Quinn says. "You have to answer. When I say your name, you have to answer me."

Maddie laughs. "You said 'fuck.'"

"You have to answer me," Quinn says again. "It's dinnertime. Come eat."

Maddie's detached and quiet as she often is after hours of reading, and Quinn thinks she won't miss her at all if she leaves.

"I'm going to go out a little," she says. She feels immediately sad about it, but also, immediate relief.

"What do you mean, 'go out'?" Maddie's more present, her voice forceful, suddenly.

"I just have some things I need to take care of." She's going to the bar, half an hour, one beer, nothing—a four-minute walk, and she walks fast. She can't quite say she's going to get Maddie more presents, to pick up a few extra things for Christmas, but she hopes that's what she thinks.

Maddie looks down, and Quinn feels sorry, almost hugs her. "You can stay up as late as you want reading. Watch a show on your phone if you want to."

"I like you being here."

"One or two shows and I'll be back to snuggle you and read," Quinn says. She feels a little sick again—her stomach shifts and roils—but she smiles at Maddie, grabs hold of her, and kisses her, eyes angled toward her feet.

Maddie takes a shower while Quinn makes her face up. Maddie likes a long shower, likes to steam the mirror, so Quinn puts on her makeup in her room. She can hear her daughter singing, some made-up song to a tune she recognizes from *Moana*. She smiles at herself in the mirror, proud she has a girl who she can trust to be left alone like this. Every teacher Maddie's ever had has loved her; she's great with grown-ups, though Quinn has also noticed that she has no friends her age. Quinn mostly had no friends either, when she was her age. She didn't like having to bring kids home because her house was small and dark and she mostly made her own dinners because her mom was often working. She wonders if her mother will be nicer, better, in her new house. *Fresh start!* another woman wrote in the comments below the photo album.

"Save some water for the whales," she calls to Maddie.

"It's fresh water, mom," says Maddie. "I should save it for the humans."

Quinn puts gunk underneath her eyes and rubs it until she looks five years older than she is. She puts on lipstick and mascara. She hears Maddie pad from the bathroom to her door. "Socks," she calls. If Maddie doesn't put socks on now she'll call to Quinn in the middle of the night because she's cold.

"You look pretty," says Maddie, standing in the doorway in the fleece pajamas Alice gave her, her socks crooked on her feet.

Quinn smiles at her, reaching down to even out the socks' seams, thinking that she was once, maybe, pretty, but now she looks too much like her mother: tired, worn out.

"Can I sleep with you when you come back?"

"You're almost seven."

"You're twenty-three."

"I can't sleep with you flailing at me."

"What if I promise not to move the whole time?"

"Not possible," Quinn says.

"I won't even breathe."

"I guess, then," Quinn says, smiling. She kisses the top of her head. "Two shows, tops, and then you can flail right next to me."

7

"Everybody's starving," Alice says, pulling open the first pizza, a flash inside her brain of Quinn and Maddie laughing. "And Aunt Alice needs a drink."

Henry helps the last kid doff coat and boots, and Tess says they all need a hot bath before dinner. "They're fine," says Martin.

"They'll catch a chill," Tess says.

"I'm so hungry I might faint," says Jack.

Alice hands out paper plates, ignoring Tess, and pours herself three thumbs of bourbon.

"You guys have fun with your aunt and uncle?" says Kate, coming down the stairs with Josh.

"The most," says Jamie.

"Mommy," Bea says. Her braid is mussed and loosened by her wool hat. She holds tight to Henry. "Tell my mom how fast I went," she says.

Kate comes up to Bea and grabs her braid, unbraids and begins to rebraid it.

"So fast," Alice says.

• • •

The kids are all cross-legged on the floor with their pizza. Both twins still wear their snow pants; Colin has his hat skewed sideways on his head.

Tess stands close to Alice, talking in a whisper. It feels important to her that Alice see this whole thing from her side. She thinks about the time that she came up here, brought Alice gin and chocolate, how good it felt to sit with her, be there for her, like that. "I'm not going to rub it in anybody's face," she says. She too has a glass of bourbon. "But we've already sunk at least a hundred grand into that house over the past decade. Martin didn't want Helen to have to pay a mortgage; we had to get the foundation redone and new windows to keep the insurance low after that year with all the hurricanes. We got the roof fixed. That place sucked money. She should have sold it years ago. Of course no one told sweet baby Kate."

Only Tess and Martin knew how bad it had been for Helen, for how long. On and off in Nick and Helen's life together there had been issues around money. He had not planned for his demise so early; they had never had much savings. She had gone to college, studied French literature and philosophy, but had never had a full-time job. She would spend the ten years after her husband's death in jobs she didn't like and that didn't much like her—an assistant teacher at a preschool, a receptionist for their childhood dentist, a real estate salesperson. She would struggle not to let the children know, to continue to send them gifts and pay for school and room and board and lend them money in those early years when they still asked—the years Martin paused grad school to teach high school because he couldn't live off of his stipend and she couldn't write the check she would have had to write to convince him not to work those years until Tess finished law school and got a job and he went back. She would refuse to leave the house where they were born and where her plants were, where all their rooms were still their rooms. She would accumulate debt for years before Martin and Tess learned how much.

Alice picks a piece of pepperoni off her pizza. "It was her home, though," she says.

Tess feels a flash of irritation, regrets the "sweet" and "baby" she used about Kate. *But we're friends,* Tess wants to say. *I'm not awful,* she wants to say. *What I'm asking for is what is fair.* She takes a third sip of her bourbon. "You wanted her to sell it too," she says at last.

"I get it, though, why she didn't," Alice says. "She had a life there. Anywhere else she would have just been a mom."

"Is that such a bad thing?" Tess says.

"Of course it isn't. It's just—I mean this as a compliment, but she was more than just their mom."

They watch Jamie pick all the pieces of pepperoni off his pizza and shape them into a smile on his flattened paper towel.

"Penny for your thoughts?" they hear behind them.

There is only one person in this house, Tess thinks, who would say this phrase out loud. "How's the igloo, Josh?" she says.

"The architecture," he says, "the ingenuity of those cultures is really something."

Tess looks past him toward Henry and Martin.

"Excited to show it to the kids," he adds.

"You guys find the outlets okay?" Alice asks.

"Oh yeah," Josh says. He holds up his phone. "Waze. I wanted to talk to you, Tess."

Alice starts walking toward the kitchen. "Who wants dessert?" she says.

Tess almost screams at her to stop. "Sure," she says to Josh instead.

He sidles close, and she can smell him, beer and soap and pizza. "I know how you feel, about the house," he says.

"I don't think we should talk about this without everyone." She gestures around the room—Martin sitting next to Henry at the table, talking, Kate on the couch, quietly eating her pizza, the kids all still spread out, seated on the floor.

"I don't want to make any decisions. I just want to talk."

Tess can see the front door over his shoulder. She could grab the keys hanging on the hook in the mudroom, put on her coat and boots and drive back to their apartment. Leave the kids here with Martin. She could sit, quiet and alone, until they've performed all their precious rituals and Martin and the kids can come back home.

"Then talk," she says. "I guess."

"I think you know what this means to Kate," he says. "What Helen meant to her."

"I'm not sure what you want me to say to that."

"You understand, though? What I mean by that."

"This doesn't have anything to do with how much any of us loved Helen."

"Sure, but . . ."

"It's money, Josh. An asset. You're familiar with the process of inheritance. It's not possible to split a house in three."

"We could set up a payment plan," he says. His chin is narrow. He has a fine film of day-old stubble on both cheeks. "We could pay you all, over the next decade. As soon as we get settled there."

"We all have expenses," she says.

"As you say," Josh says, sitting up a little straighter, "you also have a job."

Kate watches Josh talk to Tess from across the couch and wants both to tell him to stop and to urge him to keep talking. She watches Tess's posture, the way Josh sits farther forward in his chair.

She pulls off the twins' snow pants as they each eat their third piece of pizza. "You guys have fun out there?" she says.

"The most fun," Jamie says.

"Jack, use your napkin, not your T-shirt."

"When does Santa come?"

"Tomorrow night."

"You guys want cookies?" Alice calls from the kitchen.

"Yes please!" both boys say, jumping up.

Kate walks across the room to her brothers.

"I can't talk without my lawyer present," says Martin as she sits down across from them.

Henry laughs, his head down toward his drink, then up at Kate. *Grow up*, she wants to say. *You're too old to laugh at his dumb jokes like this.*

"What ails you, Kate-bug?" says her oldest brother.

It's what Helen called Kate when she was little; her brothers only ever said it to her as a tease. She feels like she might cry and wills herself not to. She squeezes each knee with a hand and breathes in hard, then reaches for the rest of Martin's drink.

"Maybe you should try to think and talk more often without your lawyer's help," she says.

"Look who's talking," says Martin, nodding toward Josh.

"They've all got us by the balls," Henry says.

When Nick died, Tess and Martin were already together, but he drove up to Boston to pick up Kate from college on his own. Together, they drove north to Maine to get Henry, and then they flew out of Portland as a group. She sat between them, her big brothers. Kate was not yet twenty. She was worried for their mother, sad and scared, but also—lodged between them, both their shoulders so much higher, bigger—she had felt better, safer than she had since Helen had called to say their dad was gone.

Tess had come down for the weekend, done up and put together at the funeral, helping Helen navigate the logistics that accompanied Nick's death. But those first few days, before the funeral and the death certificate, the paperwork and lawyers, it had been the three of them. Helen was in shock, smaller and more quiet than she'd ever been; the house too big by contrast, arid, empty; their rooms still their rooms but made-up, worn-out versions of the rooms that once belonged to them. Helen hardly slept at first, and they'd stayed up with her, watching all her favorite movies and TV shows: British detective dramas, everything Jane Austen. They took turns with her, sleeping in shifts, as Kate and Martin would do years later when they had kids.

After three days of that, Helen finally slept. "I'm tired, honies," she said late one afternoon, before they'd even begun talking about dinner. "I think I'll go to bed."

Henry had weed, and Martin went to get a pizza at the place they all liked that was much better pizza than there should have been in their small Florida town—some guy who'd moved down from New Jersey. It was better pizza, even, Tess said later, than most of what they had in New York. Henry rolled a joint, and they all sat outside, and Kate found three old cans of Heineken in the extra fridge their mom kept in the garden shed. It was the beginning of the spring semester, February, but it was warm outside, and they were barefoot. Henry lit the joint, and they all smoked it. They ate their pizza folded, no plates; Martin found some paper towels. The sky was clear, and they all looked up and talked for hours about nothing. Kate got too stoned and laughed too much, and her brothers laughed at her. Martin had taken the year off from his PhD to save money and teach high school while Tess finished her clerkship. The way he talked about the kids: one of the things Kate holds against Tess when she feels like holding things against Tess is how much she thinks Martin would have preferred teaching high school. But the PhD was so much more prestigious, so much more well suited to Martin's incredible intelligence, Tess would say a few months later. *My dad taught high school and he was smart as fuck,* Kate wanted to say but did not. Henry was building his yurt in Maine. He knew Alice already, but she'd not yet moved in with him.

After, as they all went upstairs to their respective rooms, Kate checked in on Helen. She watched her a long time, asleep, alone under the covers. Then she listened for her brothers: Martin talking on the phone to Tess in a whisper, Henry passed out on top of the covers of his childhood bed. Kate felt better; she felt less shocked and scared after that.

She would still be sad and lonely for a long time. She'd take a semester off from college, move back in briefly with Helen. But that night with Martin and Henry had shifted something. It had not made any of the concrete facts of what they'd lost any better, but it let Kate know that there'd be more life after: stupid stories, long, late nights sitting outside laughing with her brothers, conversations about nothing in Helen's backyard.

She wishes now that she could grab them, get hold of both their arms above their elbows, make them stand up, take them out-side. It's cold out, but she doesn't think it matters. There's no way there's not more weed somewhere in this house. They could replace the beers with Alice's good bourbon. She's not sure even she would want the house as badly if she knew that without it, both her brothers would still sit outside with her like that.

"Alexa!" Colin yells behind them. He's standing up, his pizza half on the floor, and Kate reaches down to slide it back onto his plate. "Play 'Crocodile Rock,'" he says.

"Who's Alexa?" asks Henry.

"You don't know Alexa?" Stella says.

"You know what a Luddite is, Stell?" Martin says.

Henry sidles up close to Stella with another piece of pizza. "Your dad ever talk to you about surveillance states?" he says.

"You're like a parody of yourself," Martin says.

"We don't have an Alexa," Alice says to Colin. "You want music?"

Colin nods, looking at each of the grown-ups. "You know 'Crocodile Rock'?" he says.

"They did a thing with the song at school," says Martin, to make clear he's not the one who introduced his son to Elton John.

Alice types "Crocodile Rock" into her phone and attaches it to the speaker: fast piano, some sort of horn, that voice like no other. When Colin said the name she wasn't sure she knew it, but then—*I don't think I've heard this song in twenty years,* she says, as every word comes back.

All the kids stand and start jumping, whirling. Colin gets up on the couch and bounces up and down. Henry grabs Stella's hands and they twist their bodies, elbows loose, elastic; Henry lifts and dips her, holds one arm as she twirls.

Even Tess gets up, and the twins jump and bob their heads around her. Josh grabs Kate, who runs in place in front of Bea, who laughs at her mother, jumps up next to Colin on the couch. Stella comes up next to Alice and grabs her hand and they start marching, knees up high then down. They're sweating, reek of bodies. The fire burns and the heat's on and the last remaining sweaters, hats, and pants are peeled off. They all fling their arms, go wild.

"You in college?" The guy isn't young but he's attractive. He isn't as old as most of the guys Quinn sees in town. She almost didn't leave Maddie but then thought better of it. She couldn't sit another night in that apartment, so pissed at her selfish stupid fucking mother, scrolling then rescrolling through her Facebook feed. It feels good to let herself feel angry, after so long being performatively good. Maybe, also, it's an excuse for just a little bit of recklessness.

"Sure," she says. "College." She's joking, but he doesn't know she's joking, so she goes along with it. She imagines him imagining her: a student, at a study group or something, in a dorm suite. She imagines he thinks this lie makes her smart. She still tracks Maddie's dad on Facebook. She never told him. He finished college this year. She wonders, each time she clicks through his pictures, if he feels the lack of Maddie somehow.

"Nice," says the guy. His skin is red and sun worn, though it's winter.

"You?" she says.

"Construction," he says.

She nods.

"No use for me," he says. "College."

"I like learning," she says, thinking now maybe she's pretending to be Maddie. She aches, just then, to go home to her girl.

"You look like it," he says. "Back for the holidays?"

"For Christmas. Celebrating with my mom."

"Just you two?"

Quinn nods. Her mom was, in fact, super into Christmas. The flutter of activity at church and the attention paid to her because she baked extra for the bake sale, dressed Quinn up: *Such a pretty girl,* they said, touching Quinn with cold hands, *her mother's twin,* they said, and Quinn had to work hard not to run away or wince.

"I'm all she has," Quinn says, thinking, still, of Maddie.

"That's nice," the guy says, nodding toward her drink: an offer.

She nods, lets him ask the bartender, Matt—who is neither mean nor nice, and Quinn likes this about him—for two more. Matt sets down her beer and eyes the guy.

"What you studying?" the guy says.

"Astrophysics," she says. It's a word Maddie uses, a thing she claims to want to be. Quinn also said it because she figures if he asks her questions to which she doesn't know the answer, she can make up the answer and he won't know.

"Fancy," he says.

"I'm into black holes," she says.

There was a thing last year, on the news, about some woman figuring out how to take a picture of a black hole. Quinn wasn't sure what the big deal was about taking a picture, but Maddie had convinced her teacher to print a copy of it on one of their special printers so Maddie could bring it home and hang it on the fridge. Quinn stares at it sometimes, making dinner, making coffee, stands barefoot looking at it after Maddie is in bed. It looks like the ocean, but what the ocean might look like were it made of shiny black. Maddie talks about being an astrophysicist, as well as a veterinarian, as well as a professional horse rider, as well as an engineer who builds solar-powered cars.

What Quinn had wanted to be, when she was younger—and this is proof like all the other proof that Maddie is an improvement on herself—was an actuary. The father of her best friend in middle school was an actuary. Quinn was good with numbers, and he talked to her about it, commented on her sharpness and her quickness when they talked percentages and fractions, said she had *a real mind for the type of work he did*. He got home before her friend's mom, who was a high-up administrator at the local hospital and worked long hours. The dad made them dinner by himself. He told Quinn to call him Mr. P. He was kind and he was steady, asked Quinn and his daughter careful, thoughtful questions. Quinn thought most about the solidity of him. She wanted the two-story house, the easy way he changed out of his suit into a T-shirt and shorts and began to cook each day at five fifteen.

"Dark," the guy says, about Maddie's black holes.

Quinn laughs. She thinks how fun it is, being her daughter instead.

8

Tess carries Stella up the stairs with Colin dragging behind her. "We'll skip bath," she says to them.

"We got sweaty," Stella says.

"We'll get you extra clean tomorrow."

"I'm too tired to take off my clothes," Colin says.

"You both have to use the bathroom."

"I can't move."

"Colin," Tess says. He still wets the bed sometimes, but if she reminds him of this he'll get angry and embarrassed. "Please," she says. "Do what I ask."

He lies down on the mattress, and she leaves him, takes Stella to pee and brush her teeth and helps her change into her pajamas. She lets her crawl into her and Martin's bed and picks up Colin, who has pulled a blanket over his head and is feigning sleep, who groans in protest as she picks him up. He's so big, she almost falls back and only does not call down to Martin because she doesn't want to call attention to the fact, for the others to see, that he's left her on her own with bedtime.

"Just let me sleep," says Colin.

"You need to use the bathroom," she says. "There is not a cover on that mattress. I can't have you pee all over it."

He gets heavy underneath her, tenser. "You're a stupid mother," he says, breaking free of her.

Tess falls back against the banister. Her hip hits hard, and the pain shoots straight up her side into her neck. Colin walks back to the mattress on the floor and pulls the duvet over his head.

Kate hears Tess's body bang against the stairs and almost goes to ask if she's okay but doesn't. She hands the kids their pajamas, finds them each a fresh pair of socks.

"I don't want to brush my teeth," Jack says.

"It's fine," Kate says.

"Our teeth will rot," says Jamie.

"One night is fine," Josh says, coming up from downstairs, a beer in his hand, his face flushed. Kate wants to take him aside to ask him about Tess but doesn't. She's not ready to be disappointed yet.

"Did we earn the presents?" Bea says.

"Not until tomorrow night," Kate says.

Josh wraps his arms around Kate's waist and kisses her cheek. He's drunk, she thinks, and is relieved by how quickly this means he'll pass out. "Daddy gets to read the book tonight," he says.

"You're not as good as Mommy," Bea says.

"Of course not," Josh says, his arms still wrapped around Kate. "No one in the whole world is as good as Mommy, but I still want to read."

• • •

"We should give it to them. Who cares?" Alice says to Martin. He's followed her outside to ask for one more cigarette. She's let Henry escape early to the barn.

"We could use the money, too, right now."

"Does it even matter?" she says. "Won't you guys be fine?"

"We paid 1.2 million dollars for this damned apartment Tess said we had to own, to have an asset. Colin's therapist doesn't take insurance. Summer camp is twelve hundred dollars a week. There does not seem to be an end to the amount of money that we need each year."

"Maybe you should leave New York."

"Our lives are in New York. And we love the kids' school."

"Maybe they don't need to go to summer camp," says Alice.

"Maybe my little sister doesn't need to be a spoiled brat."

"She's just so desperate, Kate is. How much would two hundred grand even help?"

Martin laughs. "I forget sometimes how rich you are." Alice wants to tell him she's not, really, but then, she's never had to be. She can't stomach any more talk of his and Tess's child-centered obligations. She doesn't mention that the only asset passed directly to her also has her exiled in this place she often hates.

"It's a lot of money, Martin. But it's money. It'll just disappear the way money always disappears."

They both look out toward the barn. Martin's drags are long and careful. Alice holds her cigarette between just her thumb and index finger, and her pulls are short and hard.

"What's he doing out there anyway?" says Martin. "What's the point?"

"It's birds," she says, suddenly defensive.

Martin stubs his cigarette out and puts it in his pocket. "A way to fill the days, I guess."

"He's trying to capture something that might no longer exist," she says.

He looks out toward the barn, and she looks past it toward the woods.

"What's going on with you, though?" she says. "With your job? Tess said you might be losing it?"

"I won't, most likely. It's not worth anyone's concern."

"You fuck an undergrad or something?"

He looks angry, she thinks, maybe. His eyes follow her eyes to the woods.

"Shit, Martin, I was joking. *Did* you sleep with an undergrad?"

"Of course not," he says. They finally look at one another. "Fuck you for thinking it. I talked shit about one student to another student."

"Were they female?"

"Does it matter?"

"It feels like it might matter."

"You social working me or something?"

"I'm trying to have a conversation with you."

She finishes her cigarette and stubs it, but neither moves to go inside.

"You know what my dad does?" she says, but doesn't wait for him to answer. "He trades futures. I still don't know what that means, in part because he never told me. Because he was always the sort of father who thought it was his job to go to work and so he did. But I was always super into the idea of it." She looks out toward the woods, the barn, away from Martin. She's been thinking this for a while and now she wants to talk, to put words out and see what happens once they're out. Martin is a low-stakes space to try them out. "My dad surfed when he was a teenager. *The only Black guy out there,* he used to say, laughing—the only times he ever talked about being the Black guy were when he was trying to be funny. He never really told me anything about what it was like to be him, to grow up as him. My mom hated mess and sand. Even though we lived in California, we never went to the beach. It was northern California. My dad grew up in Santa Cruz. He was smart, you know? His parents were well off, and he went to Yale. He got this big job trading futures and worked long hours and made a ton of money, and when he got home he took his shoes off at the door just like my mother wanted, he went into their room and changed out of his suit into shorts and a collared polo shirt for dinner. He made a drink for himself and my mom, and we ate. I used to think maybe she tricked him into a whole life he never even meant to have. She *told* him to marry her. There was some story about how scatterbrained he'd been when they first got together, and he made some comment about how he'd not be functional without her, and she said, *Well maybe you should marry me,* and that was it. He's spent his whole life just doing what she says and I have no idea who he is besides that. I'm forty-two. He's seventy-four."

Martin lights another cigarette and takes a single drag, then hands it to her. She nods, accepts it. "When we're young we think we'll just choose the lives we'll have, the people we're becoming, but so much of it just happens. You can live a whole life without choosing anything at all. Maybe not Henry. Maybe Henry is the only one of us who's done this, but I want us to make more choices."

Martin takes the cigarette. "If you find out how," he says, "you let me know."

He goes inside after passing back the cigarette, and Alice thinks of going driving. She's only had one glass of bourbon and she feels wired, a hard, sprung coil, no longer worn out. She watches Henry out there, working. There's still so much night to go. She lights another cigarette. If she waits an hour she can take the car and loop down to Quinn and Maddie's. She can put the windows down and let the cold air shock her, turn the music on too loud. It's the only thing about this place that she likes more than the city: the ability to move, to forget the things that make her scared and worried, forget her body, windows down.

Quinn stays longer than she should have, she will think later. She has that second drink, and, already, the man is more annoying than amusing. He'd fuck her, she thinks, but it would be no more than an exercise, a reminder for herself that she has a body, that she's something other than a mother to her daughter. She's not sure she cares to be reminded of that now. She lets him buy her a third drink because she's too tired to argue. She can imagine, fully, what would happen—his hands on her, her body being not really what he wants so much as something warm and quiet that he can get inside for a while. She can imagine all the places she might let her mind go as he enters her and then he comes and then she cleans herself and gets dressed and walks out some big, heavy door.

She looks at her phone, but Maddie hasn't texted her.

"I have to go," she says, and he stands up as if to tell her not to. He puts his hand on her waist and then her shoulder, and she flinches. He looks angry, and she realizes she's desperate to get out. She gets her coat and wonders what she'll do if he follows. She says she's going to the bathroom. She wants only to crawl in bed with Maddie. If Maddie's still in her own bed when she gets home, she'll pick her up and bring her into hers. She thinks that maybe she could crawl out the bar's bathroom window but she isn't sure if the bathroom has a window. She's had three drinks and she's not sure she could climb out a window if she tried. She walks out the front, assuming her drinks have been covered. She'll come back during the day tomorrow to make sure.

As she walks toward home, the cold is biting, sharp. She looks behind her once, then twice, then three times, that feeling in her body that maybe he's behind her. She thinks, briefly—and will later force herself to remember that she thought this—of the tramadol in her drawer inside a drawer. She thinks—and this part she'll hold tight to—this is the last time she's going to leave Maddie alone at night like this. What's better than home with Maddie? Beer, men, an hour to herself: none of it comes close to being with her girl.

Alice gets in her car and puts the windows down and drives farther up the hill instead of down toward Quinn and Maddie's. Kate falls asleep between the twins while Josh is passed out next to Bea in the bed on the floor. Tess stays up writing work emails next to Martin, who sits, chastened, after she whisper-yelled at him for not being there to help put the kids to bed. Henry scales the ceiling of the barn, back flat on the scaffolding, fastening his birds, one and then another. He climbs down after each one to check and measure their relationship to one another, to gauge how close they sit both to the ceiling and to the other birds. He wants them close enough that they look from certain angles like one fluid thing, far enough apart that they seem separate, still themselves.

Maddie's bedroom door is closed, and Quinn comes in and pulls the leftover chicken fingers out of the fridge. She takes off her shoes, stands in socked feet, pours some ketchup on a plate, and eats all three standing up, and after she feels better and more solid. She thinks maybe she won't check on Maddie—she doesn't want to wake her—but she's missed her. But Maddie's bed is empty, and she isn't in her room or in the closet, in the bathroom. Quinn checks her own room, underneath the couch, the closet next to the entrance that barely even fits their boots and coats because the landlord still uses it for storage: old buckets and mops, a small axe for clearing the backyard.

"Maddie!" she says, though the apartment's small and she knows by now that her daughter isn't in here. Absurdly, she checks every kitchen cabinet, half hoping Maddie somehow folded herself into one of them like she did sometimes when she was little, half hoping that Maddie might come in from outside and find her like this, that she might come up right behind, laughing, thinking what a silly mother she has, saying, *Mommy, what are you doing? I'm right here.*

Quinn texts her. Baby? Come home. Please baby come home.

There's no one she can call. Quinn can't stop thinking this. If anyone finds out Maddie's not here they'll take her from her and won't ever give her back.

Maddie's coat and boots are missing also. "*Madeleine*," Quinn says again, in the middle of the kitchen. It feels less scary when it isn't quiet; hearing her daughter's name out in the air is better than hearing only the silence of her not being here.

She opens the door to the apartment. It's still so cold, and she breathes in one sharp breath.

"Maddie," she says, but quiet again, because she doesn't want to wake the neighbors. Because the neighbors, just like the cops that she can't call, just like anyone she might think of who might help—they could just as likely take her from her. They could just as likely make it so that she might never see her little girl again.

"*Madeleine,*" Quinn whispers over and over. She walks through the parking lot, her breath quick. She has no gloves, and her fingers are already cold and stiff as she clutches her phone, checking. She keeps thinking that this space of time in which she feels shoveled out again and can't quite breathe and her head feels like someone is pressing hard against it, on top of it, that this time will soon have passed.

A hundred feet in front of her are woods, dark and thick. The Hudson is five hundred feet past that. There's ice out there, chunks of it. Maddie likes to go and watch it, the way it collects and cracks and travels down the river like tiny sideways boats, all white and yellow. When Madeleine was very small she used to ask if she could ride them, and Quinn was always worried, if they got too close, she'd dive in. She'd disappear.

Maddie drags the axe she found in the closet by the stairs, and her arms ache and her shoulders are stiff and tired. The axe is heavier than Maddie'd thought when she set out. She carried it at first like a huntsman, lodged between the curve of her neck and her shoulder, but now she pulls it behind her with both hands. She meant to find a small tree, to cut it down and drag it, surprise her mother: a gift she got all on her own that they could share. Kevin cut down his own tree in *Home Alone*. She meant to be back, to have the tree in the house before her mother ever knew that she had gone to get it. She shouldn't have told her that they couldn't have one and she feels bad about it now. Why not give this small thing to her mother? That picture from Alice, the tree at her house: lit up, gorgeous, *festive*. She'll be a little late but she can still surprise her. Her mom won't be mad once she sees what she's brought home. They'll get lights with lots of colors. They'll make the ornaments themselves. And it's so perfect out here, the way the air feels clean and sharp, the way the snow sits, white and blank and not too dark.

She's climbed a ridge, because a tree that she thinks that she can cut and carry has proven harder to find than she'd thought when she set out. She's not scared, though, not tired. She loves the way the moon glints off the snow, the way the quiet feels so open but also all filled up. She grabs hold of the trunks of trees as the path gets steeper; she clutches the axe with just one hand, and her shoulder aches, and her gloved hand slips on the wood, and she falls down. She's higher up now, and the stars are so bright, all around her, fewer trees as she gets farther. She thinks maybe she could lie down, right here, now that she's fallen. Her coat is good and thick, her gloves are waterproof, and maybe she could put the axe down, rest a while. Clouds are moving slowly toward her, behind the mountains past the Hudson, lit up at the edges by the moon. She could catch a full view of the stars if she just lay down right here; she'll get up again right after, find her mom a perfect tree, get home.

The Woods

Quinn is cold and sweating. After hours of searching, she's back home; she kept thinking maybe Maddie'd gone back home, was stuck outside at the door. She kept thinking maybe someone called the cops. She thinks her only option is to call Alice to come help her. If they take Maddie from her this time, Quinn feels certain, they will not ever give her back. She does not deserve to be a mother, Quinn thinks. She should have called someone as soon as Maddie went missing. She's scared, and Maddie's alone, probably cold and hungry. But there's no one she can call who won't also threaten, once they've found her, to take her from her. Alice might well do this too.

She drafts eleven text messages before she settles on the one she thinks she'll send to Alice. She almost presses send, then walks through the house one more time and finds Maddie's phone under her bed. She sees, there, a text from Alice of a Christmas tree. It's perfect, big and full and gorgeous, and Quinn feels the fury rise up in her. *Bitch,* she whispers. She sits on her daughter's bed and throws the phone against the wall.

. . .

"Maddie?" says Alice, hardly thinking. It's early morning. Her phone rang, and Maddie's face popped up, and she answered, excited, then embarrassed by how quickly she'd picked up.

"It's me," says Quinn, her voice shaking.

"What's wrong?"

Alice waits, her upper back and shoulders tensing, as she hears Quinn start to cry.

"You okay?" Tess asks Alice, still sweating, just back from her run. Kate comes up into the kitchen, sleeves rolled from putting the turkey in the basement oven. The kids and husbands—besides Henry who's in the barn, working—are still in bed.

Alice sets the phone down on the counter, places both her hands on the back of a close-by chair. "Maddie," she says.

"Who?" Tess says.

"My . . ." starts Alice. "A girl. A case of mine. She's missing. Since last night."

"Is something wrong?" asks Martin from the entrance to the kitchen.

"Her child," Kate says, then reddens. She turns to the stove, starts making breakfast.

"A client of mine is gone," Alice says.

"Do they live close by?" Tess says.

"About three miles," Alice says, her voice steady. "In the condos close to town."

Kate holds her hand over the pan, waiting for it to heat up.

"Do you . . ." Tess starts. "Is it possible she's with the dad?"

"There is no father," Alice says. "I mean—there was, I guess, but he's not around."

"Is there any reason she would run away?"

"I can't . . ." says Alice. "I can't imagine where she'd go." Alice thinks briefly, abashed, that if Maddie ran away she'd run to Alice. She knows better than to say this. But her eyes wander toward the backyard, thinking maybe, any minute, she'll see Maddie bounding toward the door.

Kate looks outside. "It's warmer," she says, "than it could be."

"She's been gone almost six hours," says Alice. "I should call the police. Quinn should have called the police."

Josh is downstairs now too and looks at his wife, then Alice. "One of us should call the police right now."

"But if I call the cops," says Alice, "she'll lose custody."

What no one talks about but everybody knows—in the ways that families know things, in this case because of Helen (who would have never known if not for Henry, who called and told her), who called and told the rest of them, who took Alice aside more than once and tried to reassure her it was not her fault—everyone knows that a year ago Alice reported a mother for leaving her kid alone while she was at work. Alice was supposed to do this—report people who left their children, even if they were going to work—and the mother lost the kid. *The system*, Alice did and still does mutter to herself when she thinks about it: it is not meant for sustenance or maintenance, not meant to keep children with their parents; it is punitive and unfair. She thinks about this each time the job proves again how limited her ability to help is. These are the few times she thinks she might want to burrow back into art and not be so exposed every day. Three days after the state took her son from her, the mother killed herself.

"We need to help her," Kate says, whisking the eggs.

"Yes," Tess says, annoyed she wasn't the one to say this. "We should help her look."

"I'll take you," Henry says to Alice. He's come in from outside in just his jeans and T-shirt. Martin must have gone and told him.

"I'll come," Josh says. "I have a headlamp in my car."

"It isn't dark," Tess snaps.

Kate looks at her. "Tess and I will stay back with the kids."

Josh and Martin go upstairs to get socks and sweaters. It's so gendered, all of a sudden, the Men going out to find, maybe to save, this little girl. Tess cuts thick slices of bread, eyes angled toward the children; Kate rolls the eggs slowly in the pan.

Alice is grateful no one stops to think more. If she just keeps all of them moving, acting, doing, maybe no one will bring up calling the cops again.

"It's going to hail soon," Josh says.

"We'll pack coats," says Henry. "I have a stack of umbrellas in the car."

"Scary," Kate says.

Tess jumps and almost says she's sorry, but then instead they both pretend she didn't jump. She resents the men, as they pull on their coats and boots. It's self-delusion passed to them not just structurally but chemically: entitlement so deeply embedded they believe they can help solve any crisis. Their boots bound loudly out the door, keys and phones and wallets shoved in hands and pockets. Tess butters toast, then puts on jelly, puts it onto plates, and passes them to Kate to spoon the eggs over.

They pile into Henry's truck, and Alice can't figure out why Josh and Martin won't stop talking. She hates how thrilled they seem, *invigorated,* while she can hardly breathe. *Maddie's missing,* she wants to scream in each of their faces. But they don't know her, this girl Alice loves but cannot talk about because she's not hers.

"I can't imagine it," Tess says.

They both stay quiet, watching Colin grab his plate, then the twins. They both know, of course—yesterday morning, with Colin; every time at the playground when they couldn't see them; those times the sitter did not immediately text back; sitting in the chair at the dentist, phone far away in their bag; running an errand, accidentally leaving the phone on the counter, reaching a hand in an empty pocket the whole time—both of them have spent every second that their kids have been alive imagining this type of loss.

Henry's mostly quiet, driving. He looks at Alice a few times; she looks down, hot-faced, as if he knows, all of a sudden, that she loves Maddie more than she loves him. Josh goes on and on about *establishing a perimeter*. Alice feels certain that all the language he's throwing out is straight from the hours she knows he spends—instead of helping with the children—*unwinding from work,* watching *Law and Order: SVU.*

The roads all wind, and Alice feels nauseous. She's prone to car sickness, and usually when she and Henry drive together she's the one to drive. She's still not used to all the trees, the quiet, the looming mountains. When they started telling people they were moving up here, all anyone said was, *It's beautiful,* or, *It's so quiet.* When had everyone gotten together and decided these two things were valuable, necessary? If this were the city, and Maddie had gone missing, someone would already have found her, some kindly MTA employee would be waiting with her until Quinn arrived. Out here there's no end to what might happen, what might snatch her, sting her, maul her, what she might have fallen from.

The kids all eat their breakfast, hardly talking. Tess keeps looking outside toward the woods, the barn, the street, where cars are coming one after the other. She looks at Kate, who looks at the children, down at her plate, her inert phone.

The sun is rising higher in the air when Josh, Henry, Martin, and Alice all file out of the truck. Quinn comes toward them. She looks small and young. Alice is twenty years her senior; Alice could, in fact, be Quinn's mother. She wants to help her, make all of it better. Also, though, she wants to hold her by her shoulders and scream in her face, *What did you do?*

"It's okay," she says, as Quinn crumples into her. "We'll find her." She feels the men's eyes on her, wondering, she thinks, why she'd make this promise. Why she'd say this thing that might turn out not to be true.

Quinn stiffens and backs away. "She took her coat," she says. She's stopped crying and is staring, clear-eyed, at Alice, eyes darting briefly to the men. "I thought for the first few hours that she had her phone. I have it, though. She left it here."

Alice keeps her eyes toward the floor, thinking briefly, shame-facedly, of all the texts she's sent.

Tess and Kate bundle the children up and take them outside. Tess is terrible at this part of parenting, the less clear, less structured parts: going outside *to have fun.* The boys immediately begin to fight, something about a shovel someone's found that they all want to use, and Tess feels unmoored, unsure how to referee or who to take aside to talk to sternly, but Kate calls to them all that she has come up with a game: the older kids can be the sled dogs, she will be the sled; Jamie and Jack can be the drivers and ride on her back. Of course, the boys want to be dogs as well, and all five children mush and trudge on through the snow, howling and barking, happy, and Tess watches the strength and heft of Kate's body, the way she bounds through the snow and the kids pile on her, and thinks she seems so much more capable, more powerful than Tess has ever been.

Quinn thinks, for the first time in a million years, that maybe she should have called her mother. These people cannot help her. She thinks of all the times she's opened up her phone and scrolled in search of someone who might help.

A plan is hatched somehow. The men ask questions. Henry looks back and forth between Alice and Quinn. Alice stands close to Quinn and touches her three times—once her shoulder, twice her arm by her wrist. Quinn flinches only the first and second time. She stands separate from them and says Maddie likes the woods and this is where she thinks she went but this is also where she's spent the whole night looking for her. There is no naming of the Hudson, which is so close Quinn thinks that she can smell it, though she would not be able to say what the smell is. Soot, wet dirt, whatever fish smell like when they're frozen under for the winter; maybe, also, what she smells is fear. Everybody's phone is charged, the men say, and Josh and Martin will go in opposite directions in the woods on trails out toward the water; Henry will go up the mountain that's part of a state park. Quinn and Alice will walk Main Street; most stores are still open, and they'll look for Maddie subtly, not wanting to attract attention. They'll climb the hill on the other side of town, will walk to the woods behind the school that also connects up, three miles straight through, to Alice and Henry's house. The plan is that they'll check in via text message every half hour, to report on their progress, any leads (Josh's word), and, regardless, they'll meet back here before dark.

Henry hands each of them a big umbrella.

"Might be a storm," says Josh.

Quinn crosses her arms over her chest and feels Alice watch her: "Do you want . . ." Alice says, starting to take off her scarf.

"I'm fine," Quinn says.

· · ·

Kate takes Bea to pick up a few remaining extra groceries at the Food Town.

"I always forget how many eggs I need," she said to Tess, then she looked sorry. "I'm awful," she said. "Still fussing about my precious dinner."

"We still have to eat," Tess said.

Tess takes over with the children. She figures after a couple more hours in the snow they'll be worn out enough to sit in front of the TV until this other child's found. They've started their own game, and though it's much warmer than the day before, the sky is gray and getting darker. The kids all laugh and run and pile over top of one another, and Tess tries not to think about how much time they have left until the storm. A whole half day will pass, and then she'll bathe them all together; they'll get dressed in the clothes Kate brought so she can get her picture; they'll get dressed in the pajamas she sent a couple weeks ago. It was Helen who used to send the holiday pajamas, every year after Thanksgiving.

When all the kids are in their holiday pajamas, Tess will turn on an especially long movie and help chop things for Kate while they split a bottle of wine and pretend to like each other more than they do. Tess will try very hard not to bring up the house. As soon as they find this missing girl—because Tess has chosen to believe completely that this girl will be found—they'll all celebrate and toast each other, toast the small ways they can still care for and love one another, no matter how awful at it all of them are.

• • •

Alice can't think of what to ask Quinn. *What were you thinking* will not work, nor will it help find Maddie. *She'll be okay,* she wants to say, but can't.

"I shouldn't be allowed to be a mother," Quinn says. "They were probably right to take her from me when they did."

"She loves you," Alice says.

"Why'd she leave, then?"

Alice has no answer for that. She looks straight ahead and tries to visualize what finding Maddie will feel like. She tries imagining the feel of Maddie close to her again.

"I love her," Quinn says, and now Alice sees that Quinn is crying. "She's all I have."

Alice thinks that she should pull her to her, that she should hold her arms and tell her that they'll find her, but she doesn't. They're all implicated, Alice thinks, in whatever happens to Maddie now.

Up close, Tess likes Kate's children better. Colin has so much fun, really, when his cousins are around. Stella gets annoyed with Bea and comes to sit with her. She's too big to sit on Tess's lap, but Tess pulls her up. Their coats swish and smush as Stella settles in.

"What's happening?" Stella whispers.

"It's almost Christmas," Tess says. "We're all together."

"But something's happening. Daddy and Uncle Henry left because something's wrong."

Colin falls, and both twins pile over top of him. Close by, the igloo sits untouched. Tess considers daring the boys to try and push it over, cave it in.

"Boys," she calls instead, not loud enough.

"You were asleep?" Alice says. "When she left?"

"I never—" Quinn starts. Then she stops, pauses. "I left," she says, not looking at Alice. "I put her to bed; she reads all night. I went out for half an hour."

Alice clenches both fists in the pockets of her coat.

"I was—" Quinn says. "She had that phone."

Maddie was one of Alice's first cases. Quinn had just been hospitalized, Maddie had just been removed from the home. She was living in a foster home, and the first time she met Alice she told her a joke: *Why should you never play cards in the jungle?*

I don't know, Alice answered.

Too many cheetahs, Maddie said.

Alice had laughed out loud.

With Quinn, it's been less easy—Quinn, who clearly loves her child but seems sometimes ill-equipped, so young. Alice knows that there is no father in the picture, that Quinn is not in contact with her family. She knows how very lonely, even with Maddie, Quinn must be. How very lonely—even having Henry, her mother calling, Tess texting, so much more time and space and safety—Alice has been too.

She thinks: if it were her, if Maddie were hers, she would never have left her by herself.

• • •

The twins are squealing and yelling, and Tess can't see Colin anymore beneath the snow. She sets Stella down and tries not to run or yell as she pulls them off and lifts Colin out from under them.

"Stop it," he says, angry.

"You can't be in the snow like that."

"We're playing."

"Play something else."

"Bitch," her son whispers. The twins both titter, shocked, their faces at first thrilled, then, as she stares at them, red and still.

She turns back to her son, grabs his face and holds it close to hers. He looks scared and she whispers to him: "Just know whatever you put into the world you can't take back."

The town is a single street, and many of the shops are closed. Alice doesn't spend much time here. There are four antique shops, a coffee shop, a restaurant she's never been inside with a purple sign and a poor approximation of vines that she thinks are meant to suggest Italy. There's snow, hard and gray and stepped in, packed against the curbs and on the edges of the sidewalk. In summer, the place fills up with tourists from the city and there's another restaurant, with a small porch built onto the sidewalk, that serves passable omelets and frittatas and has a line out the door from April until after the first snow. It's all empty now, most of the shops closed. They pass the only bar: the flash of TV through the dark window, the smell of cigarettes and beer.

They walk another block and pass the gas station and are already mostly out of town. The elementary school is another block up a steep hill, and the plan is to check the yard behind it; behind that is a graveyard and then acres of parks that they'll trudge through toward Alice's. The terrain back there is rocky and uneven, ridges that jut up and out. When Alice and Henry have gone for hikes, they've had to take breaks, find sticks to re-allocate their weight and steady themselves on their way down. Maddie's sturdy, though, and her center of gravity is lower. Both Alice and Henry are tall.

The school looks sad and empty, red brick with big, square windows. It's the middle and the high school too. Alice and Quinn climb the steps on the side of the school and walk through a small garden that Alice knows the town raised money to help build. They pass the basketball court, covered in snow, and arrive at the playground. They each hold one side of the metal railing. Alice looks down and sees that Quinn's shoes aren't waterproof.

The kids are sweating, and Tess brings them back inside, all of them, hot and damp underneath their coats and sweaters. It's been hours, she thinks, should be dark soon, but she checks her phone and sees it's not yet noon. Kate comes in with Bea, and they unload the groceries. Tess turns on the TV and the kids sit in front of it, splayed: Colin upside down, his head hanging off the couch, Jack's legs stretched across his brother's lap.

"Any word?" asks Kate, as if she didn't have her phone with her, as if somehow, a signal would have been sent back only to Tess.

"Nothing," Tess says.

"I guess it hasn't been that long."

"She's been missing since last night."

"Who?" Bea asks.

"Go watch the movie, duck," Kate says.

"Who's missing?" Bea says.

"No one, ducky." Kate looks at Tess as if she'll have an answer.

"Aunt Alice had to go look after one of the kids she helps," Tess says.

"Why did Dad go with her?"

"To be helpful."

"Where are her parents?"

"Her mom just needed help," Tess says.

"Go watch the show," Kate says.

"It's stupid," Bea says.

"Bea," Kate says, more sternly.

"Kate," says Bea.

Tess looks away, flinching.

"Bea," Kate says again. She pulls her daughter to her, then holds Bea's shoulders and pushes her away. "Don't be a brat."

Bea walks out.

The men stand by the water.

"If she's out there," Josh says.

Martin holds up his hand. He needs Josh not to say it. If she's out there, there is no going in to get her. If she's out there, she won't ever be found.

Josh and Martin have been walking mostly silently, Josh reading his compass, checking the incoming storm on the radar on his phone. Josh looks more competent out here than he does in the kitchen. Martin thinks Tess is so much better, generally, at executing whatever needs to be executed; he wonders if she should be here instead. He thinks the only reason she and Kate sent them was because they didn't trust them alone with their own children. Tess leaves him alone plenty with the children, but she'd never let them be alone with Josh.

For a long time, after their dad died, Martin had felt separate from Henry and Kate and Helen, if only because he'd felt like it was his job to take charge. This was wrong, of course, because it was Helen, not him, who'd taken over, but Martin, as the eldest, had felt at least as if he should try. He didn't cry like his siblings at the funeral; he didn't let their mother take him in for months as she had Kate.

For years, Martin smoked cigarettes because it was one sure thing that could make Helen angry. He was petulant like that, could be, and he wondered if it was catching up to him now. Now he looks at his family and sees them as a small good gift. They aren't perfect: they fight, and maybe none of them would have become friends if they'd not been forced their whole lives to be together *as a family*. But they love each other and they like each other well enough.

"We'll take another trail back to town," says Martin. "In case . . ."

"The mother should have called someone," Josh says. They've known each other twenty years, and Martin can't remember now a single thing he knows about Josh that he didn't learn from Kate or Helen.

"She called us," Martin says.

The twins fall asleep, which might mean trouble later; Stella and Colin and Bea lie worn out and crooked on the couch. Tess cuts apples, and Kate rolls out the pie dough.

"You think she's okay?" Kate says.

"I don't know," Tess says. "It was cold last night."

"Why do you think she'd leave?" Kate asks. "Did Alice say before this . . ."

"I don't think Alice goes in unless something's wrong."

"You think the mom . . . ?"

Tess doesn't answer. She pours the apples into a bowl and mixes flour and butter and sugar.

Kate says: "Isn't there always something wrong?"

Two months ago, Kate had called Tess crying. *I miss her,* she said. *I know,* said Tess. *Are you okay? I miss her,* Kate repeated. *I can't.* Tess was walking into court, had files in her arms, a client beside her. *Kate?* she said. *Honey? I need to call you back.* She thought maybe she would tell the client the call had been from one of her kids. Tess had called back, on her walk home from the subway, but Kate hadn't answered. She'd called again the next day: still no answer. Neither of them had brought up the crying the next time they talked.

Any luck? Alice texts Henry. She knows, of course, he would have called her. But she needs affirmation they're still out there. She wants to be reminded that more people are looking to find Maddie than just her and Quinn.

No sign. I'm almost to the river.

You think that means she wasn't out there?

I have no idea.

"What'd they say?" Quinn says, peeking through Alice's armpit at the phone.

"No sign," Alice says.

"Where the fuck," Quinn says, "could she have gone?"

. . .

"How are the kids liking school?" Tess asks. Kate knows Tess knows already that Jack has always had a hard time, that Jamie is fine, a strong reader, that Bea is, perhaps, a prodigy in math. She knows about the switch to Montessori because Helen told her, and then Kate yelled at Helen. Kate knows that Tess is trying not to talk about the house.

The pie is in the oven; the turkey, bought from a local farmer, has been cooking in the basement oven since Kate went down to put it in at five. The house feels warm and smells like Christmas, the Christmas Kate's known her whole life and wants so much to give her kids.

"We separated the boys this year," she says.

"Seems smart," Tess says. She slices the potatoes and lays them in a pan with cheese and egg and breadcrumbs, not how Kate would do it, but not awful.

"Bea doesn't have a lot of friends," Kate says. "I worry about that."

"We worry," Tess says. "It's our job."

"She's not interested in other people. It feels sad or something. A little creepy sometimes." Kate feels bad for saying this last part out loud.

Tess brushes the stray breadcrumbs into the trash.

"She just disappears when she's right there." Kate picks a piece of cheese up off the cutting board and eats it. She still has sugar on her fingers, and the flavors mix. "She throws tantrums, too, and I think she's too old to throw tantrums."

"Your brother still throws tantrums."

Kate looks at her and laughs, thinking: *not like Josh's*. "The kids are big but they're not big really. I feel like they're at this strange, hard stage where they only need more of me, except their needs are more well hidden, so it's harder for me to know how to help."

Tess nods. "I think that all the time—like, if I could just stay with Colin to remind him to pay attention and to be kind. If I could just have tattooed on Stella's arm that not everything's her fault."

Kate gets a bottle of wine from the fridge and uncorks it. "I need it for the gravy," she says, half apologetically. "But not all of it."

Tess gets two wine glasses, and Kate fills them up.

Alice and Quinn walk a path past the graveyard. It's an acre lot, no more. Old stones lean back and sideways. All the trees around are bare. They enter the marked trail, where the snow is deeper.

"Blue diamonds," Quinn says. "When we come up here we do the blue diamond trail."

Alice isn't sure if this means they should stay on it or avoid it. It's white and gray around them. The sun's higher in the sky, but the sky's filled up with clouds, and the whole world looks blank and sad.

"Mom?!?" they hear from the main room.

"Yes," both Kate and Tess say, not sure whose kid it was.

"We're hungry."

"We'll eat soon."

"We're hungry now."

"You just had breakfast."

"We're growing kids," Bea says.

"Who knows how long they'll be," Kate says, nodding toward the window.

"Come in here," Tess says. "I'll cut you up some—"

"I don't want fruit," says Colin.

"Just come in here," Tess says.

The white of the snow and the gray brown of the bare tree branches, the sound of boots and shoes in snow: Alice thinks all of a sudden that maybe she should paint this. That one day, when all of this is over, she'll make a small charcoal of this scene; she'll give it to Maddie. She thinks maybe, when this is over, she'll take Maddie home with her; how could Quinn think, really, after this, that she should be in charge. Immediately, Alice feels sick and sad for thinking this, but also, it niggles in her body, in her brain, as she walks next to Quinn.

"You were smart to not become a mother," Quinn says.

Alice thinks that if she buries her, right here in the snow, no one will know; no one will look for her. She'll find Maddie by herself.

The kids have two bags of chips Tess found in the pantry. Stella has a peanut butter sandwich—she never gets peanut butter at home because Colin is allergic and Tess won't allow it, and she's only let her have it now because she's in a chair across the room and promised promised promised that she'll wash her face and hands as soon as she's done—and Bea has a bowl of the leftover apples cut up for the pie.

"My life is mostly making snacks," Kate says.

Tess laughs.

"I envy you, though," Kate says. "Having a place to go, a reason to put on a bra."

"I envy you all the time you get with them," Tess says.

They're both lying. Kate knows Tess often misses bedtime. Tess can't fathom what she'd do at home all of the time. Once, before she had kids, at a firm dinner with one other female lawyer and three of the male partners and their wives, one of the wives told Tess she was thinking of going back to work as a teacher. She said: *You can only unload the dishwasher so many times.* Tess has friends who stay home, and they do lots of other things that maybe she'd do also: they cook and meet for coffee, go to museums, write postcards to politicians. She thinks she might go crazy if she had to be alone with herself that much.

The path flattens out, and the trees have gotten thicker. The air's so sharp, it feels cleaner, fresher; the wind has picked up, branches crack and bristle. Every ten-ish minutes, Quinn hears the far-off sound of a car whooshing past.

"I wanted to be a mother," Alice says.

Quinn stays quiet. She's dumb, she thinks. Always assuming. Almost every time she talks when she's with Alice, she thinks later she would like to take it back.

"I wanted to be a mother," Alice repeats. "But I couldn't."

"I'm sorry," Quinn says. Stupid, pithy. Quinn's the one whose kid is missing.

"All I wanted was to be a mother for a long time, and now I feel like maybe I'm just nothing since I'm not."

"You helped us," Quinn says. She feels silly saying this, annoyed she still feels obligated to be nice.

"Of course," Alice says.

They've reached the top of a hill and can see bare trees and snow but no Maddie.

Where the fuck is Maddie? Quinn thinks; she feels so close all of a sudden to crying, or to falling, the not knowing, all the blank where Maddie could be stretched out and white and gray, and Quinn is scared. She can see Maddie's tiny body, how it looks solid even up close—stout legs and arms, that perfect belly. But also, how little she still is.

Quinn grabs hold of Alice's arm without thinking, feels Alice loop her arm in Quinn's.

"We want to go outside," says Colin.

He smells grown-up, sweat and chip grease.

"We're trying to make dinner," Tess says.

"We're bored," he says.

"We can watch them out the window," Kate says.

Tess feels her body clench, but the kids are already piling toward the mudroom to get their coats and boots.

The clouds have gotten heavier and darker. Tess opens the mudroom door and feels a gust of wind come through. "I don't know," she says.

"*Come on,* Tess," Kate says. "It's the backyard. Just let them go."

Tess holds tight to her wine and drinks what's left while watching the kids pile out the door, the clouds blue and gray and purple. Behind her, Kate goes back in the kitchen toward the stove.

. . .

"I need . . ."

Alice wants to ask Quinn not to ask her. She wants to say without saying that she'll protect her, that she won't report her. She wants not to say it in case later she decides she wants to take it back. She wants to be good at her job, to see through to another side in which Maddie and Quinn are people that she serves, a family that she helps, and not something that she wishes she could keep for herself. She thinks again of Laurie, the other mother whose kid she took from her, the way her hands were folded in front of her chest, pleading, desperate, the way they fell, limp and helpless, to her side when Alice told her she'd have to remove her son.

"I love her," Quinn says.

"I know you do."

What Alice doesn't say but thinks: *What if you're still not enough?*

"What is it?" Kate says. The prep is done, and they sit now together in the kitchen, perched on stools, their elbows resting on the wood-block island. Kate pours them both another glass of wine. "What makes you so scared?"

"What do you mean?" Tess says.

"You're so *on* them." Kate takes two gulps of wine.

"You're saying this while a little girl is missing."

"She's Alice's charge for a reason."

"So then it's this woman's fault? That her little girl is gone?"

"Of course not. This isn't that. I'm just saying, if your kids skip a bath, they won't die."

"Kids need structure," Tess says.

"Sure. I just . . . kids need independence also. It doesn't always have to be so hard."

"It's different," Tess says. "When both parents have jobs."

Oh, fuck you, thinks Kate.

Quinn should have seen it coming. Their arms are no longer looped, and there's a layer of ice under the snow, and when Alice slips she falls out of Quinn's grasp before Quinn knows her feet have lost hold. The upper right side of Alice's head catches on a low-hanging branch, and the skin on her forehead rips, is broken open. There are stark red blotches on the snow, blood from her head, before she's even fully planted there.

"Fuck," says Quinn. "Alice." She doesn't want to have to be the grown-up. "Alice, are you okay?"

"Fuck," says Alice, her hands in the snow, staring down at the bright red.

"What are your parents doing for Christmas?" Kate asks, which is a way to hurt Tess that can't be held against her later on.

"They're with my sisters, I guess," says Tess.

This always shocks Kate, to remember that Tess has sisters, when she's obviously so bad at it.

"Annie puts them all up at her place," Tess adds. "My mom loves it. Annie's so rich."

But you're *rich,* Kate wants to say, though Tess won't admit it; Tess is one of those rich people who likes to say she's *middle class.* Kate blames New York for this—no matter how rich you are, there are plenty of people in the city who are richer.

"How's Colin this year?" Kate asks, which is another dig, sub-tler, but also, she likes Colin and she hopes he's doing better.

"They want us to medicate him," Tess says.

Kate nods. She has thought before, if she just waits to see what Tess does, what the doctors tell her she should do with Colin, maybe then she'll know how to help Jack.

"I'm just afraid," Tess says. "If you read all the books, every-one is sure except for you. Like, one guy says it's abuse not to medicate him; another says it's administering amphetamines to children—which it is—which a lot of people get addicted to. Some say it's the beginning of the ride to opioid abuse. I read this book that said that kids in West Virginia and Virginia, all the kids addicted to opioids, they were taught at a young age that drugs were the answer, so then they just took other ones when the ones the doctors gave them didn't work. Maybe it's capitalist bullshit, but then, these are the systems that we're stuck with. *I'm* capitalist bullshit. I can't just wait for him to fail, you know?"

"What do you think, though?"

"I'm not a doctor."

"You're his mother."

"I think the only way to actually keep him safe is to never let him out into the world."

"Are you okay?" Quinn asks again. Her face is so much like Mad-die's.

Alice's forehead stings, her whole head aches. It's a strange sensation, watching the blood drip from her head; it's bright and vivid. Her wrists feel sore; they twisted as she fell and they're raw from the snow. She reaches up again to touch the blood.

She hates her body, she remembers briefly. Her body is a failure, and this is only further proof of that. She's the one with the good shoes. *The grown-up.* But then here she is: on the ground. As if the fact that she's older, trained to provide comfort and safety to other humans in moments of extreme duress, is worthless, really, in the face of a patch of ice and this small branch.

You're going to get wet, she thinks, staring at Quinn. She thinks maybe she should scold her. If she scolds her, she'll feel more like she's in charge again.

"We went to Starbucks, the other day," Kate says. She feels bad now. She shouldn't have brought up Tess's family, Colin's medication. They're on their third glass of wine.

"The drive-thru wasn't working," she says. "I drive half an hour out of the way to go to the Starbucks with a drive-thru so I don't have to get them all out of the car. I spent hours driving around when they were little, did you know that? They only ever slept in the car, and I would drive for hours. It was the only time of day I really liked. I'd treat myself to a latte, sometimes a cookie; I'd listen to music, drive till they woke up. But anyway, the other day, I took them to my old favorite Starbucks, and they were awake but they were strapped in at least, and it felt like a break. Josh is so freaked out about screen time. I told them we were doing errands, which means nothing to them except that probably we'll drive a while, and I decided to treat myself to a latte like old times. But the fucking drive-thru was closed—who even closes a drive-thru? I guess it was broken or something. So we had to go inside. Bea's in a booster now, and she got out on her own while I climbed into the back to get Jack, who sits in the third row because otherwise he kicks the other two. So I got them all out, and no one got hit by a car, and I was relieved but also I was yelling the whole time. A young couple gawked at me—you know the way people do when they don't have kids yet, and they look so certain that they'll do it better when it's them? We went in, and of course there was a line, and I almost walked right back out, but the night before Jack had wet his bed, and I hadn't been able to get back to sleep after, so I was beat and I was desperate for a coffee. So I bribed them. I told them that if they behaved they'd all get a treat. I use food too much probably. But maybe food's emotional regardless. So I said, if you behave for this ten minutes that we have to stay in line, I'll get you a cake pop when we get to the front. Bea's *on it,* you know? She loves the double chocolate. But the twins forget within seconds, and Jamie knocks over a coffee mug, which mercifully doesn't break, and Jack keeps running into the guy in front of us, and I grab hold of both of them and threaten that they're about to lose the treat, except I can't actually take the treat away because then they'll scream and, also, there's still so much line left. And then Jack has to go to the bathroom, and so we lose our place in line, and the fucker in front of us, who Jack really only tapped but who clearly either doesn't have kids or just doesn't parent them, looks so obviously relieved. So I get them all on the toilet and off and wash their hands, and they all manage to touch the garbage can before we leave the bathroom, and I'm sweating in my coat and now I have to pee but I don't because I don't think all three of them can keep their hands off everything for the thirty seconds it will take me, but then at the last minute I decide to, and then Jack opens the door and this older woman is standing waiting for the bathroom and I just stare at her, my pants down and grabbing for Jack and almost peeing on myself. The point is—you know. Parenting. So we get back in the line, and the baristas all look like they're about to cry, and someone's yelling because their kid's hot chocolate is too hot, and then the boys hear that there's hot chocolate and they want that in addition to the treat they shouldn't even have, and we finally get to the front and they hit each other and I'm still threatening them with not getting a treat even though I've ordered them already, and I'm paying and the barista's gone to make my drink, and, Jack—I'm not looking, but I also see him, you know, because I have to, he's not a kid that you can ever stop at least partially knowing where he is—I don't think I fully register it until later, but I do in fact see him slip two chocolate milks in my bag as I pull my card out of the machine and the barista comes back with my latte, but no one else has seen him, and I'm so fucking tired, and I don't want him to start screaming, and I just want to get the fuck out of there because everyone is looking at us, so we just leave."

Kate's face is hot now, and she can't believe how long she's been talking. The sun is lost behind the clouds, which are thick and white and blank. The kids keep running, playing, jumping; she's counted them at least a hundred times while she's been talking. *Three, four, five,* she thinks, scanning small heads over and over. *One, two, three, four, five.*

"I stole them," she says. "I just let him steal them. I am a constant, total shit show of a mother. I didn't give them to him. But I also didn't say anything to him. I let them sit in my purse all day and then I threw them away."

· · ·

They use Alice's scarf to stop the bleeding. It's still bleeding, but it's no longer a gush. It has to clot, Quinn thinks, though she can't say how she knows this. They're both still seated in the snow, and it's only now that Quinn realizes they're both soaking wet. It's started to rain. Quinn's fingers are so cold.

"You okay?" Quinn asks, which is the only thing that she seems capable of asking.

Neither of them opens their umbrellas.

"We have to move," Alice says.

Quinn's jeans are wet straight through, and her skin has gone from wet and cold to sharp and stung. Alice is also wearing jeans and she looks just as cold. Quinn thinks briefly that she should google frostbite, hypothermia, how to keep warm when you're soaking wet in cold and snow. But they don't have any other clothes, and whatever their phones tell them will not help. It's warmer than it could be, warm enough that the rain isn't ice but wet.

She thinks of Maddie, *hypothermia and frostbite*. They have to walk, one foot then the next.

Alice's hand is on her scarf, stopping the blood. Quinn stuffs hers deep in her coat pockets to get warm. She tells herself they just have to get back to the house and hope that somehow in the meantime Maddie's found. That she's okay, that, even though this woman tasked with taking care of both of them has fallen, is hurt, that Maddie's somewhere out there and she's fine. She's dry and safe and warm.

Tess thinks that she should touch Kate, hold her. She wants to tell her that she, Tess, is a cold, withholding asshole and that's the only reason they aren't closer, that it is absolutely not Kate's fault that Tess is mostly too closed off to feel close to anyone.

Quinn tries not to let Alice see Quinn looking at her. Alice's face is drained. Her arm holding the scarf up to her head looks thin and limp beneath her coat. Quinn's not sure how far they are from Alice's, though she's driven slowly past it. She found Alice's address online, and it felt only fair.

"Why would she have left?" Quinn says. What she is thinking is that it's raining, and they can't see well through the rain. If Maddie is out here and wet, if she fell like Alice did, what will happen to her then?

"What were you guys talking about yesterday?" Alice asks.

Quinn thinks briefly of her mom. "Space," she says.

Alice checks her scarf, which is soaked now, takes off her gloves.

"We're not going to find her," Quinn says.

Alice stays quiet while she holds the scarf back up to her head. "We're close to my house," she says, finally. "The rain will stop."

"This girl I know," Tess says. The wind picks up again, and they watch the kids watch it. The wetness in the air has raised the temperature, and Colin and Bea have both taken off their coats. It's started to rain, but neither Tess nor Kate has gone outside to tell them to put the coats back on. Tess hopes the little girl is somewhere warm.

"I don't even know her," Tess says. "We went to high school

together, and she was much cooler than me. This woman, not girl. Her baby died. I saw it on the internet. I don't ever go on Facebook, and then one night I couldn't sleep and went on Facebook, and there were all these posts. Like there was some alert because of how many reactions or comments or whatever. It was a car accident. You don't actually think about car accidents. Or I don't. We hardly ever drive. I'm so scared to fly but I never think about the car as dangerous. We spend so much time pretending that they're safe, but they aren't. The fucking world is burning, and we spend all of our time worrying about whether our kids will get into the right schools, summer camps, whatever. We spend so much time worried that something awful that we can't name will happen, but then we mostly ignore all the very real things that are everywhere, that we know are just in front of us. All those times I was texting in the car. Those fevers they had that went too high, but it was the middle of the night and I didn't want to bring them to the doctor, I was too tired to go to the ER. When they fall and hit their heads and you just hope—you read that shit about how, actually, concussions aren't as specific or as consequential as they sound. Anyway, this girl I know, she was a cheerleader in high school. It doesn't matter, but we weren't friends. We're in our forties; I haven't known her since we were seventeen. We've probably had five or ten conversations in our lives, and we're Facebook friends. And then her baby died, and she was posting all this stuff about her grief on the internet. Going through it for everyone to see. It fucked me up, I guess. I had to stare at it all the time—at work, at home, making dinner. Stell and Colin would be right there in front of me, alive, completely fine, and I'd be scrolling through the condolences people had written to this woman for a kid I'd never even seen, and sometimes I'd start to cry. I'd grab hold of the children—I probably scared them. I'd tell them I loved them. And they'd look at me like kids look, you know, when they think you're acting strange. *Sure, Mom.* Colin has gotten pretty masterful at rolling his eyes. I looked at this little girl over and over. She was twenty-nine months old. I thought about what that might be like, tried to imagine each of those months, all the months and years after. I looked at the dad's Facebook and the aunts' and uncles'. Grandparents'. I envied this girl, in that vague way all girls envy girls like her in high school. Small and thin and pretty, you know? Her husband was driving when it happened, and I watched a whole year wondering if she'd leave him. They had an older child, another girl. The mother posted about her grief for months and then suddenly she went quiet, and then when she came back she started posting about all the ways that her baby was with her—in a cloud or rainbow, you know, stuff I don't believe in. But I wanted to believe that she believed it. I was addicted to it. Until I guess I wasn't any longer. I haven't looked at it in months. It was all I thought about, and then work got busy. Summer started. Kids, life, blah blah. It wasn't quite real—and yet . . ."

She picks up her phone again as if maybe she'll check on this woman right now. She thinks of Alice and Martin, Josh and Henry, out there, but no one's called or texted; her screen is an old picture of the children, two years younger, hugging one another, making faces. She sets the phone back down.

Kate passes her the wine bottle.

Tess pours her glass full, and they both stare out the window at the children. Bodies piled over bodies. They can't hear them, but their mouths move, laughing, squealing, maybe screaming.

"It's luck," Tess says, her eyes set on the flush of one of the twins' cheeks as he runs close to the window. "The whole thing. Dumb fucking luck."

"I'm golden, with a purple mane and tail and a horn that shoots lightning," says Stella. It's raining, but the kids don't care.

"I'm that too," says Jamie.

"No copying!"

"I breathe fire," says Bea. "And ice!"

"I'm the ruler version of the birds that Uncle Henry made," says Colin.

"You're not my ruler, though," says Bea.

"Everybody has to have wings," says Stella, "so we can fly."

"And sleeping darts," says Jack, reaching behind his back as if he had a backpack. "So we can *smite* our enemies."

The rain stings both their faces. Alice thinks she needs Quinn to walk and not to think and so she talks. "The fourth time I was pregnant I named her," she says. "I wasn't far enough along for anyone to tell me the sex—who knows. But in my head they were all girls. I named her, the fourth one—Penelope. After this writer. Anyway. I said the name sometimes, out loud when I was by myself. I had learned to be better at not hoping, but I still did. It was so stupid, but I did. I saw friends and walked around the city. I went to my studio and sat for hours imagining her. The last thing that I painted was her, them. I mean, I never saw them. It was swirls. I painted after Penelope and before the last one. It was so obviously wrong, two dimensions and a bunch of colors.

I understood for the first time how very little what I made could hold."

What Alice doesn't name is the shame that she felt so often at the end, before she quit. All those years of all those predawn hours. All those years of pots of coffee and paint stains on her fingers, her whole body aching from the work, not able even to hear what Henry said when she got home. All those years of her head down and smiling and pretending when she went to parties, angling for her work to get shown. And then to have her dreams come true: a show, attention, positive reviews—to see so clearly all at once: some mentions in a section of the newspaper that hardly anybody read; all those people at her opening, their plastic glasses filled with wine, their empty nods; and none of it adding up to anything, no one seeing, grasping, truly understanding what she spent so long making, so long laying out. It was the babies but it was also everything around her—all that talk with Henry about the climate, reading the fucking news, people dying, suffering, and her still pouring everything she had into paint and form, tearing up and gluing together canvas scraps: the extraordinary shame she felt when she finally saw how little, really, her work mattered. How embarrassing, to have ever thought that it might matter; how little any of it was worth.

"I miss her so much," Kate says.

"Me too," says Tess.

Kate had promised herself not to lionize Helen after her death. She had, at various points in her life, and to the detriment not only of herself but also of her relationship to her mother, lionized

Helen while she was alive. Helen was a forceful presence, whip-smart, well-read, loving. She was also critical, too quick to assume, often very loud. In high school, Kate had hated her. This was unsurprising—mothers and their daughters—but Kate's hatred had felt deeper, purer, than that of her friends. It was the first time she'd been able to glimpse her mother not as caretaker but as rival: her mother picking books for her, picking clothes for her, because of what these choices might say about them both. Her mother was an intellectual in a place where no one valued intellectuals. She loved this about herself, and Kate did not. Kate wanted only to be like all the other girls, her mother to be like all the other mothers. She hated her mother's commitment to, her investment in, *quality* and *taste*—what Kate thought of and saw, at thirteen, fourteen, fifteen, as ways to alienate herself. But then, of course, she got older. But then, of course, her mother was—and who could say things like this as a grown-up person without feeling embarrassed, infantilized, but also, Kate and Helen thought and said it proudly, not least to one another—Kate's closest friend.

"She was so fucking loud," Kate says. The kids are still outside playing, and it's warm inside. "She never didn't have an opinion, was always in our shit. I think I thought when I moved away I'd have some sort of buffer. It was one thing to talk on the phone every day, another to have her coming over to tell me I shouldn't leave the house without a bra on, taste testing my lentils, telling me the dinner I made was bland. But then I missed it. Like some sort of masochistic baby. Her voice felt so much a part of me that I didn't even need her in the room to know she thought my fucking food was bland." Kate sits quiet, looking out the window; the children running. *One, two, three, four, five,* she thinks. "I know you all think I'm silly. Josh says I have to move on. It's boring, how sad I am. Just about everybody in the world has to survive losing their mother. And how fucking lucky we were to have her. She used to ask the girls in my class who weren't my friends to be friends with me. We'd see them at the grocery store or the beach or something, and she'd introduce me to them, as if we didn't see each other every day and they just didn't like me. They liked *her*! They didn't even know her, but they liked her, and she'd pull me over as if she could force them to be my friends after all. She was on my side, I guess, is the point. Which, like, again—sure, fine, who cares. But she's the only person in the world who ever saw me the way she saw me, who loved me like that, who remembered me as all the things I'd ever been and also thought of me as all the things she still thought I might become . . . It feels harder—fucking *terrifying*—that there is no longer any person in the world who loves me like she did."

"Stop it!" Bea says. "We're not supposed to run that way."

"Let's go to the barn," says Colin.

"I don't like it there."

"We need a cave," says Stella. "We need somewhere to trap our enemies."

"I used to take the train down to the city on my days off," Quinn says. She knows Alice is trying to distract her. She puts one hand on Alice's arm and loops her other arm around her waist. She still doesn't like her. But they're out here together. She thinks maybe if she talks long enough about her daughter, Maddie will appear. "This lady," she says, "used to watch Maddie when I worked, but I never knew what I was supposed to do with her all that other time. I had a good stroller someone gave me, one of my old coworkers at the restaurant got it from her rich cousin. I took the train down to Manhattan. Off-peak. When the conductor came by I'd nurse Maddie and, if it was a guy, he'd just say no worries, he'd come back, but he'd never come back. I took her to the Met because you got to pick how much you paid and I'd pay a dollar. The ladies at the desks sometimes would look at me funny, but what the fuck did they know about my life. I spent hours in there. I'd never been to a museum, at least not one like that. I wanted her to have all that stuff inside her. Like, I thought it would just stick. I thought maybe then she'd think she was a person who had a right to stuff like that. It sounds dumb, maybe, but you know that big room with all the sculptures and the light? In the front, when you first walk in, there are these little-kid statues chasing birds that always freaked me out. But I'd sit in there, take her out of the stroller and face her forward on my lap. I thought she liked it. I guess it's like your job to think your kid is smart; she couldn't even talk yet, but I was pretty sure she got it. I thought she'd explain it to me when she got big. She'd babble a lot at the hieroglyphics, the big old portraits. Those weird ones? Jean Dubuffet? She had opinions. Just like she still has opinions." Quinn almost smiles. "Fuck," she says. "Fuck fuck."

What Quinn doesn't say is that that whole time, on those trips to the museum, Quinn was also going to the city to buy heroin. She could buy it close by, too, but she went down there so she would buy it less often than she wanted. What she doesn't say is sometimes her dealer asked to hold her daughter, and she let him. She left Maddie in the room and went into a bathroom and shot up while he did. That he was completely fine, a person; Maddie almost never cried when she left her with him; she was only gone a small amount of time—but that then, like now, she'd pretended not to acknowledge how often she needed, wanted, to get some time away. Ignoring the consequences. What Quinn doesn't say is that sometimes she hates being a mother, even as she loves Maddie, and she's worried now that that's why Maddie's gone. She doesn't tell Alice that she thinks maybe she was a better mother after she shot up. She doesn't tell her that addiction is compulsion, an act of filling all the gaping holes where love and care might be but are not. She knows that she's already failed Maddie. Even more shameful, though, than the ways she's failed, the ways she knows she always will: somewhere, far away, the thought exists inside Quinn's brain that if Maddie's really gone, then Quinn can finally fully disappear herself.

Stella is the fastest, Jack right behind, then Colin, then Jamie, then Bea. They bound and trudge, and both twins fall, and Colin grabs the back of Stella's coat to slow her. *Stop!* he says. *Wait for me!* Bea helps the twins up, and they are once again all five bounding forward. *Where are we going?* Jack says. *We're flying!* says Bea.

The clouds have gotten darker, thicker. They're bright somehow, because it's still daytime, but Tess hasn't seen the sun for hours. Sometimes, in Florida with Helen, swimming in the ocean, Tess would get a rush of fear: when she couldn't touch the bottom, when the kids weren't within her reach, even though they both knew how to swim. She'd have to still herself, to focus her eyes on both the kids and remind herself to stay steady, to call to Martin to keep his eyes on them so she could go back to shore. She'd call to Helen and to Kate and Alice, tell them she was going running and could they help Martin—trusting herself least of all to keep anybody safe—and then she'd leave them, change into her sports bra and shorts, and go for a run all by herself.

"I was jealous of you," Tess says. "I guess. It's all so predictable. But she was yours." The wine bottle is empty. Tess has her feet up on the stool next to her; her arms are wrapped around her shins. She says, "I don't understand intimacy. I'll always be pretending. I was jealous of how entitled you all felt to her—like you just knew she would make herself available to you if and when you needed. I probably bitched about it to Martin, but mostly I was just so blood-spittingly jealous. Mostly I just wished that she was mine like that." Tess doesn't look at Kate. She wants to tell her the truth, but she can't do it if she has to remember Kate's right there. "I was proud, I guess, too, that I had to do everything all on my own. But that didn't mean I didn't envy what I thought was the ease all of you had." She wants to correct this because it's not quite right. Of course she had help, all sorts. Her parents paid for college and for law school; they loved her, in their way. But she couldn't talk to either of her sisters without feeling like they were in some competition in which only one of them would make it out alive. The love among them all was complicated, stunted, sometimes painful. She didn't blame them, but when she saw Martin and his siblings with Helen, she understood how far from that they'd always been. This was not tragic, was the main thing. She'd yearned, she saw now, sometimes in her twenties, to be tragic. But she'd long since lost interest in waiting around to be saved. She won't say this part out loud to Kate—she's not quite capable of saying shame out loud. But what she wants Kate to know is that Helen was special. What she wants Kate to know is that, even as Tess and Helen got close over the years they spent together, Helen was not ever, could not ever be, Tess's mom. There's something irrevocable about what it must have been to have had that. It's alive inside of all of them—Martin, Kate, and Henry—something strong and sure and solid that Tess will never have.

Alice is lightheaded. Maybe it's not from blood loss but from what Quinn is saying, from the way her desperation's only gotten thicker since they started walking, her fear has only gotten more intense. There's so much white in front of them. The ice has hardened on top of the branches, and the snow sits on top of that. Bits of it drop down on them as they keep walking. It's afternoon now, and the sun is high up in the air, and Alice thinks that if Maddie's made it through the first night, there's no way she survives another one. She can't tell if she's holding on to Quinn or Quinn is holding on to her. Her hands and her wrists ache. She reaches up to touch where the branch hit her and the blood is hard and crusted, already scabbing over. Her body, working, she thinks. She walks faster.

Quinn speeds up with her. If she doesn't speed up just like Alice, if they don't keep hold of one another, she, maybe both of them, will fall again.

• • •

They smell the smoke before they see it. They've been so busy keeping one eye on the children as they're talking, they forgot to keep an eye on the stove. Kate had meant to check it every ten minutes; she doesn't know this oven. Her dough is particular, specific.

The fire alarm goes off, and they're both up. The smell of burning is strong all of a sudden, sharp and acrid. They both run to the stove, and Kate reaches in to grab the pie without a hot pad. She burns her palms and fingers and the pan clanks against the counter, the crust already black and crisp.

"Fuck," Kate says. "Fuck. Fuck."

Tess looks at her, then at the pie, which seems now to be crisping further.

"Fuck," Kate says again. She starts to cry. It was, of course, Helen's recipe. The apples she chose specially from their farmers' market in Virginia, half sweet, half tart. She peeled all of them herself, only letting Tess and the children chop. When she ran her hands through the sugar and the butter, mixing, adding the corn starch Helen always recommended, she'd felt better than she had in weeks or months.

The alarm has not stopped beeping. Her hands shake, red and hot. She picks up the pie—the glass still hot, all those apples heavy in the pan. She throws it, hard and heavy, far across the room. The apples splat against the floor and wall and bits of juice spread across one of the cabinets. The glass is thick and clunks hard on the floor before it cracks.

Tess grabs one of the stools from the island to climb up and stop the beeping. She grabs at and untwists the fire alarm, but it won't stop. She pulls at the batteries and takes them out, but that just causes another, slower beep that's just as loud.

"Fuck," Tess says, and throws the fire alarm against the wall as well.

The way the rain falls—steady, not quite hail, but cold and close to frozen—Alice has stopped registering it as wet so much as just the way her skin feels now. The snow gives more when they step than it did an hour ago. Shots of cloud and sky pop through the lines of branches, a blank, flat gray that only further brightens up the strips of white along the trees.

They think of the children at the same time. The smoke has spread and thinned, but the smell lingers. The broken pan and pie still splattered on the floor. Tess has hold of Kate's shoulder but turns her body so she can sneak a look outside. She's finally gotten the smoke alarm to stop.

The children aren't there any longer. Tess stands and scans the length of the yard and the garden. The barn lights are off and the rain comes down in sheets and she can't see where the children are. She hears the cars out front on the highway and she screams the names of both her children and she and Kate run outside without their coats.

Quinn knows that it's Alice's house because of those times she's driven by here. She knows the barn, which looks different from the back than the little bit she saw when she drove by, curling her neck, going slowly—all the curtains kept wide open—thinking it was only fair, when every bit of her life was something Alice had already seen.

Tess and Kate run out to the road as if there wouldn't have been squeals and screeching, tires, metal, glass, and sirens, as if their own bodies wouldn't have cracked and broken as soon as the children were hurt, but they're not there. The street is just a street, with cars driving past, the sound of ice and water splashing under tires. They look up and down in both directions, then run out to the back. They hear them soon enough, but it takes a while to figure out where they are.

"The fucking igloo," Tess says.

Jamie pins Jack against the snow, and Bea and Colin burrow a hole beneath the inside wall, and Stella, who saw her first, sits cross-legged, face wet, hands in pockets, thrilled that there are now as many girls as there are boys among them, and asks her if she wants to play stinging birds and alicorns.

They're a pile at first, and neither Kate nor Tess sees her. The kids are laughing at them, silly, frantic mothers. *We were right here the whole time. Can you believe we all fit inside it? Look, Mom,* one of them says. They're not sure which mom the kids mean.

We found a girl.

She looks cold, but no bone or skin is broken. She looks tired. Her face is red, lips chapped. *Resilient,* Tess thinks, which is what her favorite teacher called her when she was in law school and which she stopped believing she was long ago.

"Madeleine?" Kate says.

The girl looks up at her, and the kids all stare like they never would have thought to ask her name.

Josh's igloo has lost half a wall, and the lights are on upstairs, and Alice hears Tess as they come up past the barn. Alice reaches in her pocket for her phone and sees she has ten missed calls from Tess that she must not have felt because her hands and hips are numb.

"She's here," Tess yells.

Alice looks at Quinn, not willing to hope yet.

"Madeleine," says Tess. "Alice, Madeleine is here."

Alice stands there shocked, her forehead throbbing, afraid that she'll start crying, and watches Quinn run into the house and up the stairs, and she stays still and listens as Quinn makes a sound unlike any sound Alice has ever heard a person make.

The Birds

The men trudge back toward their cars, embarrassed. Of course they're glad the girl's been found but they each lament in their own way that they weren't the ones to find her. Henry's careful, driving through the sheets of rain that's begun to turn to snow. He leans forward, shoulders clenched and hands tight around the wheel—even Josh isn't talking. His headlights glint off the wet and fog, and he can hardly see.

Inside the house, Kate stripped Maddie down in front of the space heater in the bathroom and wrapped her up in towels and warm blankets. Tess googled *frostbite, hypothermia;* the Mayo Clinic warned against the shock of hot water or a heating pad. Kate got the girl a glass of water, found chips and fruit, and Tess rubbed her arms up and down over the blankets that they'd draped over her arms. She seemed both more and less strong than any of the other children. Her limbs are leaner but they look better held together, hard and firm. She looked straight at them in the bright light of the bathroom, and both Kate and Tess had to work hard to look straight back.

Kate left Tess with Maddie and ushered the other children into her room. She stripped them down, too, dried them off with towels. She found them fresh clothes and brought them downstairs with the promise of more food.

The girl's lips are chapped and her skin is sharp with cold, still. She's not said much but she stares at Tess. Tess fixes her eyes on the girl's bright red, tightly fisted hands and grabs hold of them with both of hers. *My mom*, she said once, and then a second time, while they were outside. *Can you please call my mom?*

The mother is a child, Tess thinks, as she steps back, as the mother-girl barrels past her and holds her daughter. She brings in snow on the boots that she still wears, the wind and wet from outside and the cold. Her face and head and pants are wet, and Tess looks behind her, toward the door, for Alice, aware she's accidentally witnessing a thing that they shouldn't have to share.

Alice unwinds her scarf as she walks slowly into the house. It's soaked through with blood. The bones in her hands are fiery with cold. She doesn't want to see Maddie before the force of wanting to hug her has lightened enough that she can see her and not grab hold of her.

"What's happening?" Bea says.

"Who yelled?" asks Stella.

"It's fine, ducks," Kate says. "That was Madeleine's mom."

"She looks like a teenager," says Colin.

"She's not," Kate says, though she's not sure.

"Teenagers can have kids," says Stella, and Kate goes to the stove to get her sweet potatoes boiling so as not to have to answer whichever questions come next. Upstairs, she hears what she imagines is the mother scream again. Alice looked pale and lightheaded, wet and worn out, and now, after Kate finds another bag of potato chips in the pantry and hands it to the children, she goes in search of her.

She catches Alice by the stairs, holding a scarf covered in blood, and Kate's been a mother just long enough not to gasp but grabs her arm.

"What happened?" she says, and Alice points up to her head. It's deep but clotted, Kate sees. The skin around the gash is bruised and also bloody but, she says to Alice, still holding her arm, "I think you'll make it through."

She helps Alice slip out of her wet coat and pull a towel around her. "You need to strip down," she says, pulling her through her own house toward the fire. She leaves Alice there while she goes down to the dryer in the basement, where earlier she saw a pair of Henry's sweatpants, and when she comes back Alice slips out of her pants and into Henry's, into one of Kate's sweaters from the back of the couch.

Alice hears them up there: Quinn crying, Maddie's voice, no words that Alice can make out.

"Can you grab me the hydrogen peroxide from the bathroom?" Kate calls to Tess. She sits Alice down cross-legged by the fire.

Tess brings cotton balls, too, and Alice watches Kate work, cleaning, careful. Alice hears the kids come out of the kitchen, watching, asking questions. She can't turn her head to look at them; Kate is holding her chin firmly as she works on her.

"She's okay," Tess says to the children. "Aunt Kate, your mom, is taking care of her."

Quinn isn't cold any longer. Her hands are warm from holding Maddie, from helping her get dressed, but also somehow still cold, hard and aching, in the bones. Tess swept through with dry clothes for both of them, so many towels. She's wearing what she thinks might be Alice's pants now, a long sweater. Alice gave her a pair of underwear that still had the tag on.

Quinn thinks, still holding on to Maddie, that she'll have to ask Alice to let her keep her. She can't imagine anything so perfect as her daughter—her pink, flushed skin, her hands. She wants to sweep her up and hold her, to take her home and fold her into bed with her and not ever let her out. But instead they go downstairs, and Maddie breaks free of her and starts playing with the other children. She's wearing one of the other girls' clothes—Quinn can't remember which one, can't quite place their names, though she was told. They've asked them to stay for dinner, though Quinn wants to run, to pack Maddie in a car— whichever of those lined up in the driveway is parked closest to the road—just like she did that day her mother caught her us- ing, to drive and drive until it's just the two of them for good. She thinks, first, she'll stay and let these people feed them, let Mad- die sit in this warm house until they're both steady enough to go.

She sits down on the couch as Maddie and the children settle into some game with Magna-Tiles and small horses. Tess gave Maddie a grilled cheese and a large glass of milk as soon as they came out of the bathroom, and Quinn keeps a glass of water by her side that she offers to Maddie each time she comes close. She also has a bowl of cut-up fruit, potato chips, a granola bar, slices of pork, all of which the women gave her, but Maddie's brushed her off to play with the other children each time Quinn's tried to get her to eat more. *You must be so tired,* she said to her. *I slept, though,* Maddie said, *in the igloo. I'm fine,* she keeps saying to Quinn, though Quinn can't yet stop feeling scared. *It was warm in there.*

She hears Maddie declare something and watches as the other children listen to her and she almost starts crying. She watches Alice through the opening to the kitchen. Alice seems not to want to look at Quinn or Maddie. She touched Maddie once, an awkward one-armed hug while Quinn stood close by. She whispered to her, quickly, calmly. She saw Maddie whisper back. She wonders now about what each of them said. She thinks of what Alice looked like with that blood on her face, all those babies that she didn't have, her wanting and not getting. How that might be why she didn't tell on her, why, maybe, she won't.

"You warm enough?"

Quinn jumps. *Tess,* Quinn thinks. She keeps forgetting. The woman stands up so straight it makes Quinn try to sit up straighter too. "Yeah," she says. "I'm good."

Quinn pulls her feet up underneath her on the couch, then stretches them back out, apologetic. She fists and unfists her hands. She hopes this woman will go back into the kitchen with the other women, leave her here alone with the kids. Tess seems to consider sitting, but instead takes the crumpled blanket off the couch and folds it. "Let us know," she says, "if you need anything at all."

"How is she?" Kate asks.

"She's so young," Tess says.

"She's twenty-three," says Alice.

"I couldn't do shit when I was twenty-three," Tess says.

Alice and Kate look at one another. Tess was editor of the law review then.

Tess waves a hand in the air: *It's not the same.* "I lived off canned tuna and frozen corn," she says. "I mixed it every night with ranch dressing. I could not have kept another person alive."

"She hasn't had an easy time," says Alice. What Alice doesn't tell them is the way Quinn looked the first time she met her: young and desperate, sorry. She'd been discharged already, but Maddie was with the foster family, and Quinn sat mostly quiet on the couch in their dark condo by herself. Alice introduced herself at the front door. Quinn had nodded, let her in. It was intimate, what she did. It was alienating, the way Alice was meant to monitor, to make choices about whether or not she thought Quinn was fit. She thought sometimes, secretly, as she walked around people's apartments, peeked into their refrigerators, noted the cleanliness of their floors and bathrooms, how her own body had proven her not up to the task of parenthood.

"I can show you Maddie's room," Quinn said, after a while of not much talking. She was the manager at a local restaurant but was looking for something in the daytime, more aligned with

Maddie's schedule. A few weeks later, Alice would help her find a job at the front desk of a law office. Quinn's still there.

The room was small but cheerfully decorated, *thoughtful*, Alice put in her notes. There were books in neat stacks on the floor, a small, tightly made bed. The walls were painted a bright yellow with blue polka dots.

"We did it together," Quinn said. "Me and Maddie. The dots."

There were pictures of them all over the house: Quinn and toddler Maddie, baby Maddie by herself. Alice thought about these often after. She wondered if Quinn had had them printed after Maddie had been taken from her, if she had spent whole days after she'd been released from rehab taping all those pictures of her daughter onto cardboard, onto one long piece of yarn hung in the hall.

Henry doesn't ask about her clients, and she seldom talks about them, least of all these two. At work, when she overhears her colleagues swapping stories, it always feels a little gross; it's strange, though, jarring, to hold these moments, these other people's maladies, to have no way to get them out.

"The bird is almost ready," Kate says.

"Smells so good," says Tess.

Martin comes in and puts his hand on Tess's back, kisses her briefly. "What can I do?" he says.

"Sweet potatoes," says his sister.

Kate pulls the spinach casserole out of the oven, and Tess replaces it with a cookie sheet of brussels sprouts, of red, orange, and purple carrots all seasoned and oiled, fresh thyme and basil crushed on top.

"What a day," says Martin.

"I'm just so happy," Kate says. "I'm so glad everyone is safe."

They all look at one another, and Alice moves so she can see through the opening toward the children and tries hard not to answer, *For now*.

Tess runs her fingers through her wet hair, pulls it up, and puts on lotion, one for underneath her eyes and another for the rest of her face. She swipes mascara on in case Kate wants to take more pictures. She wears black pants, a green turtleneck. She wrangles both the children, freshly bathed and flushed and easy, into the clothes Kate bought for them. She fastens Colin's bow tie, zips Stella into her dress, brushes their hair.

Colin grabs Tess's cheeks and holds her, so close that she can smell the sour of his breath. He looks at her to the point that she gets hot and wants to pull away. "I like your face," he says.

She grabs him back, brushing her lips across his forehead. "I like yours too," she says.

Kate fixes both boys' bow ties, zips and pulls at Bea's dress. Josh comes in and asks her what he's meant to wear, and she tells him; he gets dressed just as she wants. She watches as his thumbs fasten the last buttons, and she thinks again that it was him, his igloo, that saved that little girl. She gets out the sport coat that she brought him, though she imagines none of the rest of the men will be wearing jackets. "Just bring it downstairs," she says. "I'll get Tess to take our picture, and then you can take it off."

• • •

In the shower, Alice leans her back against the unclean tiles. Hot water runs into her cut and stings, but she stays still, reaches up to touch the skin around it once. Her hands still ache from the cold. The water pounds and scalds. Her shoulders fold. She scrubs her body, face, and hair and stands a long time, her head back and her eyes closed. She places her hands on the soft skin of her stomach, breathing in for a count of six, out for a count of eight. *You're okay,* she says out loud, as if saying is the same as being. She says it because she knows, for now, she is.

They've given Quinn and Maddie a small room in the corner of the house to change, *to settle;* it was the sewing room, Alice told her, and then explained the house used to belong to her grandma. It had boxes of paint and stacks of books that Alice and Henry quickly cleared into the hall. There's a single window that looks out onto the barn and a small couch. Quinn thinks she will take this opportunity to show Alice how well she can mother, to be good and calm and careful. She will empty the drawer inside a drawer as soon as they're home.

Quinn holds Maddie close to her: *What were you thinking?* is what she wants to ask, how and why and what and how again. *How did you survive?* is what she wants to ask, but Maddie had that good coat Alice helped her find used online and those boots from that same place and her scarf and hat and gloves, and it was cold but not as cold as it could have been, warm enough it rained instead of snowed. She doesn't ask any of these questions. She hurls palaver at her daughter just to keep her talking, to keep looking at her. "The kids seem nice," she says. "I'll get the cookie dough tomorrow, and we can curl up on the couch, and I have a few presents waiting for you when we get home." She wants to ask more questions; she wants to listen to her, to be reminded every couple minutes that she's there.

Finally: "Why did you leave, Mad?" Quinn says.

Martin grabs Tess's arm in the corner of the kitchen—no one else is looking—and then he can't figure out what he means to say or how he'll say it. She smells good, fresh from the shower—the lotion that she uses, her specific Tess-out-of-the-shower smell. He looks at her face, which he knows better than any other person's, the freckle below her left cheekbone, the way she smirks, her eyes wide, when he grabs hold of her like this. He wants to tell her what it was like out there, how cold and white, the blankness. He wants to tell her that he missed her, though that's not right. He wants to tell her he should never have watched those YouTube videos of his student, that he's sorry for it. He wants to tell her that he's going to send the draft emails and who gives a fuck if it's not legally advisable. He's going to tell those girls he's sorry, because he is. He wants to tell her maybe he shouldn't ever go back to work, that he thinks he sabotaged his job on purpose, that maybe if he sends those emails that will be the end. Maybe he's not young enough, not smart enough; none of what he's done his whole life has meant much to anyone, and maybe he should try to find something that does. They should move up here, move somewhere all alone and off the grid where the only thing they do all day is figure out new ways to care for one another. She could start a small wills and estates firm and be home every night by four. He could stay at home and take care of the kids. Why don't people up and change their lives more often, he wants to ask her.

Stella comes bounding in because her dress got snagged when she was playing with the twins and Tess has to fix it. Bea and Colin are fighting over what they're meant to build with the Magna-Tiles. Jack hit Jamie with a toy horse. Martin looks down, breathes in, reaches for her, but Tess is gone.

Quinn stands outside the door to the other bathroom, angry. That picture of the tree that Alice sent her daughter. Now she knows who is to blame, why Maddie was gone. She stops, not sure if she's allowed her anger. She stops and waits outside the bathroom door. *Fuck you,* she whispers, but there's no point in knocking, storming in and screaming. It's a futile, useless hatred. She still knows enough to know she can't say it out loud.

Kate scurries back and forth between the dining room and kitchen. Platters, casserole trays, the bird, of course. The children are underfoot, brushing against waists and elbows. They're at her chest and saying that they're hungry, pulling on her dress, faces scrunched and hands reaching for hot plates. *What are we eating,* they say, *why are we eating that? Do I have to eat those brussels sprouts if I want dessert?*

Kate does not mind the way they pick and talk at her. It's all blunted and familiar; she can answer without thinking. She grabs hold of them, their arms and bodies, hands on cheeks, clasping shoulders. *Soon, ducks,* she says. *You get dessert no matter what.*

They're heroes, she thinks, Josh and the kids, though this is not right. But they did, her children, save that little girl. The fucking igloo. Out the window, she can see its shape has changed almost completely. The children took out one wall when they found Maddie. The temperature has risen, and the other half has begun to cave and wilt.

Her sweet husband, she thinks. He walks past, and she grabs him, kisses him, both hands on his face; he grins.

How close they were to something awful. She can't say now how thrilling it was to get close to it but not to have to touch it, not to have to feel its force. Everyone okay, the thrill of knowing, feeling fully, what an extraordinary gift their all being safe here and together is.

Alice sets down plates one after the next, her hands unsteady. She folds napkins, lays down knives and forks. *Spoons?* she calls to Kate in the other room; *Not until dessert,* Kate calls back. She sets down glasses, wine for grown-ups, water for the children. Water for the grown-ups. She fills the pitcher, slices the foil off the top of the wine and uncorks it, leaves it to breathe next to a candlestick.

Martin whips the whipped cream; Josh has been sent to pick up pies. This is blasphemous to Henry, Martin, and Kate, who were raised by Helen—store-bought pies. A woman from the farmers' market has a special table outside Food Town, and Henry's friends with her because he's friends with all the farmers, and she said she had a couple extras, and everyone decided it was best to send out Josh. Tess cleaned up the other pie, which had been on the floor, splattered, a little, on the wall, and now there is no trace.

"Duckies," Kate calls. She's leaning over, lighting each of the four candles. Her dress, a rich green velvet—a present, a few years ago, from Helen—pulls and braces, tight across her chest and back. The matches are the nice kind: the big, hard box, the large, red, rounded tops. She likes the hard press of thumb, wood to cardboard, the snap and pull and burn, palm rounded as she makes contact with the candle's wick, and then the thrill of all four of them alight. Someone has plugged in the tree lights, too, and the only other sources of light are the two lamps behind the living room's half wall. Kate will not think about her pie on the floor, and if she doesn't think about it she won't cry. She is grateful that Tess cleaned it up before she had to look at the leftover mess of it.

"Stell?" says Tess. "Colin?"

"Dinner, everybody!" Martin calls, going into the room where they're all playing. He throws one of the twins over his shoulder, and the boy laughs, and Tess watches and is grateful that he's hers. The kids all tumble after him into the dining room.

"What are we having?" asks Colin.

"Christmas dinner, silly," Kate says.

"But Grandma Helen isn't here."

"Aunt Kate cooked this year," Tess says, grabbing hold of Stella.

"Grandma Helen—"

"We did it together," Kate interrupts. "Just like Grandma Helen said we should."

Tess thinks of her first trip down to Florida, how she'd dreaded it for weeks. How she'd asked Martin a thousand different questions about what to bring and wear and how to talk in order that they should like her. How she made him stay in a hotel.

They're just my family, he kept saying to her. As if that didn't necessarily portend some sort of altercation, as if that were a word filled with something sturdy, nourishing, instead of what she knew.

Her clothes had felt too fancy. Her shirt was silk, and it had wrinkled, and she'd sweated through the armpits. Helen had taken her aside and asked her about work, and she had tried hard to figure out the sort of answers that might most please her. Helen touched her three times, a hug when she arrived that Tess had accidentally dodged and then stiffened under, apologetic, moving unthinkingly away—Helen laughing at her a few years later; *You were like some feral cat,* she said—she'd touched her arm while they talked, telling her something that Tess had realized a beat too late was meant to be funny. Tess had told her about the pro bono work the firm did, about the cases she took on that she thought Helen might think meant she was good enough for Martin. Even as she knew she wasn't, felt so sure she was too cold and broken to be folded in with all of them. But Helen didn't seem to be testing her so much as she seemed *interested.* She wore you down with all the talking, until you were too tired, until you just answered what you thought instead of what you thought she might want. The third time Helen touched Tess she had hugged her as she and Martin left, and Tess had felt the most prepared, looser from three glasses of wine and all the food, glad for all the ways the night had been easier than she'd feared, grateful for how it had felt like a way of being in the world she'd never known before.

They all climb onto the benches on either side of Henry's table, and the children argue only briefly about the seating. Kate's had her kids make name tags for everybody—palm-sized Christmas trees and elves—and Martin rearranges one and then another until they're all happy with the person that they're seated with. Kate lists in her brain as she scans the table and the food all the ways her meal is less than what her mother's would have been. The sweet potatoes look sadder than her mother's, not as well whipped. The spinach casserole looks sunken in the middle, wet with grease; the eggs have not quite set. She knows the replacement pie is being hidden from her. And then she realizes everyone else is sitting and trying not to stare at her.

Tess grabs Kate and pulls her into her chair. "Sit," she says. "It's perfect. Sit."

Kate can't quite believe this happens, but: Tess squeezes her hand.

Henry cuts the meat, and Alice watches. This important job has been his since their father died. His dexterity, Helen used to say, was always something. *It's a sort of art,* Helen would say, and then Alice would watch Henry's spine rise up as if he wanted to respond, but then she'd watch him settle back as he remembered this was just Helen. *It's an offering,* she said, which is what art is.

Alice watches Colin stuff cranberry sauce into his roll and eat it. She watches as the sauce lumps onto his shirt and he lifts his shirt into his mouth and licks it off. Maddie is right next to him, but Alice can't yet watch her. She's hardly looked at her since she was found. But she has been close enough to sense her, caught glimpses of her, small and safe and warm. She keeps thinking, *safe*, and then, for a second, she can't breathe.

"Can I have another roll?" her nephew asks.

Alice smiles at him, the skin around his lips bright red. "Sure, kid," she says, and lifts a warm roll from the basket, puts it in Colin's hand.

"So," Josh says, "A toast. To warm, safe, happy kids."

The adults all raise their glasses, and the kids follow. Colin spills his drink, and Maddie offers him her napkin. "Jesus, Colin," Martin mutters, and they all watch as the boy starts, his face turns red. Tess takes her napkin off her lap and clinks her glass hard against her husband's; she gets up to help Colin. "To warm, safe, happy kids," she says.

Tess hugs Colin, and she feels Madeleine close to them, watching. Madeleine has hardly spoken, and Tess feels Quinn watching too. No one has said much about what happened. Alice looks desperate. Tess watches as she sips slowly from her wine glass, grabs hold of the table, the tips of her fingers changing color, like before. She's leaning toward her food but she's not eating.

The whole time Tess has known her—even in the time when she lost each of the babies, when Tess brought her gin and chocolate—she's always thought of Alice as stronger than the rest of them. Alice has seemed impenetrable to Tess, beautiful and brilliant and also immune from all the petty things that madden Tess. Of course this cannot be true; whatever Alice feels, whatever she is not, in fact, immune to, Tess just figures she must share those things with Henry, though sometimes Tess wonders if Alice keeps it to herself. That is, mostly, what Tess does. Except, she thinks, what she's held all these years, it comes out regardless. She worries about its weight and sharpness. She thinks about her mother's hands holding her foot, both her sisters sleeping separately in their rooms, the cut and sting, the popping up of blood. She thinks next week she'll call Alice. Maybe, once the kids are back in school, she'll ditch work early and come up with gin and chocolate.

No one tells the children that they have to eat a vegetable. Jack is strangely obsessed with the spinach casserole and has four servings, and Colin finishes his fifth roll. Stella's always had a sensitivity to textures and picks slowly at a piece of turkey. She lumps the potatoes and the casserole into their own separate square-shaped mounds and presses on them with her index finger, and no one tells her to stop playing with her food.

They're all so dressed up, Quinn thinks. The boys are wearing bow ties, and the girls have matching dresses. Quinn has never fully understood this, even though her mother used to do it too: to put on nice clothes, to sit here with the same people that you sit with every day, as if it made you better, proved something about the value or the sanctity of this meal that you had together, which really was mostly just like all the other meals. Quinn thinks it's silly, really, except she likes the way the shape of the room has shifted, the way the candles make all of them look looser, warmer, better somehow than they did before.

She wonders when and how to ask if Alice plans to tell on her. *To tell on her,* like they're all children, tattling, like they're all at the mercy of authorities larger, more nefarious than they are. She thinks Alice won't, but also, she wants to be sure. She wants to take Alice aside in some hallway of this big old house and make her promise that this secret will stay theirs. When she left her mother's house and went out on her own, she thought she'd find other people, better than the ones that she was born with, but that had proven harder than she'd hoped. What were the rules for loving people who were not obliged to love you? How did you know when and how to trust they wouldn't destroy you too? She needs Alice to trust her now. She needs Alice to break the rules for her. Alice has, already, not called the cops, as Quinn asked her not to do. She thinks maybe this means that she'll protect her. She needs to think how to remind her that this is protecting Maddie too. How to ask her, though, how to make sure she remembers, make sure she won't later hold all this against her, how to make sure that they stay always, her and Maddie, but also Alice, just as safe and warm as they are right now?

After dinner, Tess unpacks the pies into pans as if Kate might forget they aren't homemade. Henry comes into the kitchen and catches her. "I'm making gin drinks for the adults," he says. "A fucking day, huh?"

"A fucking year," she says. She keeps thinking their lives will settle, somehow, into something they might not have ever been.

She keeps thinking that the ache of Helen not there won't be quite so constant or so sharp after a while.

Henry nods and looks past her to the dining room, where someone laughs and a fork clatters against a plate, glass clinks. "You think she's okay?" he says. Tess knows he means Alice.

"I think she will be," she says. Though she has no idea.

"That girl," he says.

"It worked out okay," says Tess, not wanting to talk about the ways they are now implicated.

Henry nods. "I guess it did."

Tess grabs his wrist, looks at him. "It's fine," she says. "If you think we should let them have the house, who gives a fuck: it's fine."

"I'm not sure the two of us can just say that."

"I'm the bad one, the cold, withholding holdout," she says. "We can put them on a payment plan."

"You're sure, though? I mean . . . I know Alice doesn't care."

"I'll get something drawn up. They can pay the four of us a mortgage. There's a way to do it so we all still benefit."

Henry looks at her, and Tess has to look past him. "You're not bad," he says.

"I still wish it wasn't fucking Josh."

They both laugh, and Henry hands her two of the drinks and leads her back out of the kitchen. "We'll put Bea and the boys in charge of the snail kites."

They go back into the dining room, and Tess and Henry pass out the drinks, and all the grown-ups thank them. The kids watch them. Quinn is meant to be a sober person, Alice has told Henry, and is not handed a glass.

Tess goes back in the kitchen and brings out the pie. Josh mans the whipped cream, sneaking spoonsful into the mouths of all the children, who laugh, talk with massive mounds of cream still in their mouths, spill on their dresses and their ties. Kate has not yet gotten her picture, but she laughs the loudest, watching them.

"My dress is dirty," Bea says, sorry.

"It's fine, duck," Kate says, wetting her napkin. "It's all completely fine."

"Another toast?" says Martin.

"To Mom," Kate says.

"To Mom," her brothers agree, looking back at her.

"To Grandma," Stella says, and raises her glass and clinks it against Colin's. The kids all cheer, including Maddie. Quinn smiles, eyes still on her daughter, hands still in her lap.

"Let's go out to the barn," Alice says after dessert, bits of pie piled on plates and whipped cream spread across Kate's cloth napkins, cranberry and gravy stains on the tablecloth that she brought back from Helen's house, and Henry looks at Alice, and she smiles.

Later, as they go to bed, Henry will thank her. Later, they won't have sex, but she will let him hold her for the first time in a long time, and it will feel good instead of awkward. She will let his arms wrap around her and won't feel suffocated. His feet will brush against her ankles in the way that at other moments she has been annoyed by, that, at other moments still, she will ask him to avoid. But this night he will thank her for suggesting that they all go out to the barn after dinner to see his birds, and she will say it was a pleasure, exactly what they needed, and she will mean it, and he will be grateful to her, and for the whole night they'll sleep close together, limbs and bodies overlapping, quiet.

"Of course," Kate says, and puts the boys' ties back on, wipes the whipped cream off Stella's dress with a wet napkin. "Maybe we can get a picture too."

Tess helps Jack and Kate helps Stella, and Colin, Jamie, and Bea all put their coats on by themselves. Quinn and Maddie put on their coats too. Josh gets the booze from the table and some glasses, but then leaves the glasses and passes the bottle to Martin, who sips straight from it and smiles at his brother-in-law as Henry leads them out. The rain's gone, and the sky is clear.

As the kids bound toward the barn, Colin takes his coat off and Martin catches it, and Bea does the same and Martin grabs hold of hers as well.

Alice grabs hold of Quinn as Maddie runs up ahead with Stella. "I need you to promise it won't happen again," she says.

Quinn nods. She looks at Alice. "Okay," she says. She squeezes Alice's arm and keeps hold of it as they keep walking.

"I am clearly not . . ." Alice starts. "I can't be your caseworker anymore."

Quinn lets go of her arm.

"I don't have to give a reason," Alice says. "No one has to know about this, but I can't—it's okay, she's okay, but it's not okay what we did."

Quinn nods again, hands at her sides, eyes still tracking Maddie.

"We can still . . ." Alice starts, but they both know they can't, that they won't ever be friends.

"She left to find a tree," Quinn says.

"I fucked up too," Alice says. "I should never—"

"Neither of us should," Quinn says.

Alice looks straight at her, and both of them stop walking. She holds both Quinn's shoulders and thinks, again, how very young she is. "You won't ever again."

Inside the barn, sheets are strung up on the ceiling to cover what's above them.

"Lie down," says Henry.

The floor is wood, unfinished. Tess doesn't check for splinters. Everyone does as Henry's asked.

Alice is next to Maddie without having meant to be. Quinn is on the other side. Kate's by Bea; the twins settle in below and beside her. Josh lies on Kate's free side. Martin holds Stella's hand, and Colin loops one leg over his mother's, who pulls at the neck of her turtleneck as she settles down onto the floor.

"Should we close our eyes or something?" Kate says.

"Sure," says Henry.

Stella and Bea close their eyes slowly, and the twins shut theirs so tight their faces start to hurt. Colin puts his hand over his eyes. He watches, though, through the slats between his fingers as his uncle pulls the closer sheet down and—though he only helped that little bit yesterday morning, though there's no reason maybe to feel what he feels—Colin feels proud.

The birds hold a breathtaking sort of birdness. There are loads of them, a hundred at least—years of work—and they sit in a swoop. A murmuration. They look like movement though they are not moving: the way their wings stretch and dip, the way their bodies are all angled slightly differently; they look suspended, in flight, all together in sync but also each themselves. They feel like birds, which maybe is the point, although they are made, Alice knows, with toxic materials—cadmium yellow, manganese blue. Henry must think it's for the greater good. The birds are small yet somehow vast, delicate and broadly reaching as a unit. Alice thinks again of Henry's hands working to shape them, and she feels a thrill.

Quinn lies a little awkward, her arm and leg and waist pressed next to Maddie's. *The birds are disappearing* is a thing her daughter's told her, and she wants to make sure this moment stays inside her body, such that she always knows that they're still here.

Kate stands up, and all the rest of them are still and silent. She climbs up onto a stool next to the kiln and lodges her phone into the scaffolding that Henry's used to install the birds and sets a timer on the camera, and then climbs back down to get in her place between Bea and Josh.

. . .

The camera clicks twenty different times, and Josh holds Kate's hand, and she holds Bea's who holds Stella's who holds Colin's who holds Jack's who holds Jamie's and they all continue not to move, and Quinn's body is still pressed against Maddie's, and Tess still has one eye on the kids, and Martin looks at Tess and then up at the birds, and Henry watches Alice the whole time: her whole body, the way it is still so full of whatever thing it is that made him love her, whatever singular and specific formulation of blood and bone and thought that make her her— her strength, the brilliance of her, long legs and fingers; the way her toes curl under when she likes whatever she is seeing when she's looking, really taking something in, the way her eyebrows straighten out. He doesn't look at first but then he does, and both sets of toes are curled just as he hoped they would be, her eyebrows too, and a shot of something sharp and bright runs from his head down to his feet and, among all the photos, which Kate will swipe through later, there will be one in which no one's eyes are closed and no one's mouth is open, their heads aren't angled in ways that are strange or awkward; there will be one in which—the flock in flight held still—they all look up.

ACKNOWLEDGMENTS

When I started writing this book in early 2019, it was, in part, to convince myself that collectivity had value; that all the broken shit aside, it still meant something, to seek out and foster a community. I wrote the bulk of this book in 2020, revised it in the early months of 2021. Like so many people, my family and I were displaced for a good amount of that time. I wrote this book at the kitchen tables and on the couches, sometimes hiding in the bathrooms, of the family members and the friends who took us in, who lent us their empty houses and apartments, who co-homeschooled with us, who let me hold their babies and watched our kids. Thank you to Charley Todd, for a truly perfect solitary New York night; and thank you to Mae Fatto and Lucas Knipscher (and George and Agrippa), Katie Knipscher and Alejandro Strong, Colleen and Marc Weisman (and Emma and Maisie), Osvaldo Monzon and Mauricio Botero, and Marisa Strong Baskin and Duncan Baskin (and Clara and Elena). For this past year and for all the others that you've been there: thank you to Cristina de la Vega and Kenny Strong.

Thank you to Sarah Bowlin, for a thousand things but also for continuing to help me get to do this thing.

To Kate Nintzel: never have I ever had the shit kicked out of me quite so well or so brilliantly.

To Eliza Rosenberry, for championing this book so doggedly and so lovingly.

Also at HarperCollins, thank you to Molly Gendell, Ryan Shepherd, Dale Rohrbaugh, Pam Barricklow, Ploy Siripant, and Emily Snyder.

For taking such care with the sentences (and that note about frostbite), thank you, Molly Lindley Pisani.

For reading, but also for the extraordinary privilege of regular access to your brains, thank you, Kerry Cullen, Leslie Jamison, Miranda Popkey, Virginia Soles-Smith, Elena Megalos, and Marcy Dermansky.

Thank you, Yurina Yoshikawa, Sanaë Lemoine, Eliza Schraeder, and Rebecca Taylor.

Thank you, Victor LaValle, teacher, mentor, friend.

Thank you, Karen and Sam Steger.

To Colin Drohan and Stella Cabot Wilson, for putting up with me and also for lending me your names.

Thank you to my students, for continually showing me new ways to read and think and write.

Thank you for always picking up the phone, Rumaan Alam.

Thank you to Kayleen Hartman: I did my very best to give you what you asked.

To Peter, Isabel, and Luisa: it is the gift of my life to get to know and love you every day.